Ultimate Destiny:

The Beast of the Beyond

K.J. Neale

Acknowledgements

I dedicate the *Ultimate Destiny* series to my mother, Jacqueline "Lu" Neale (1956-2021) for always loving me and believing in my dream.

I would also like to thank James "Jim" Neale, Toni Neale, James "Jamesy" Neale, Paul McCarthy, Vivien McCarthy and fellow writer H. E. McCarthy for their continued support in my journey to become an author.

I would also like to give thanks and credit to Kelly L. Hart and Kael Ardent for the beautiful cover design.

Chapter One

The Crysteors

Raevyria Blazeonheart was only three years of age when the matrons at the orphanage discovered that she was a Crysteor. Being simple people who lived in the Imperial Province of Lukiem located northwest in the Northern Realm of Luxdanion, they had no idea that others like Raevyria would one day come for her.

Six years later, when Raevyria was nine years old, the Crysteors finally came, three men to be exact. One of the men was the Prime Crysteor himself, Auraedeus Auramaedes, who was a tall, handsome, and stoic man attired in gold and silver armour who maintained an aura of fearlessness around himself. The second man was just as handsome, and fair featured as Auraedeus but with large glimmering fairy wings and attired in emerald-green robes. The final man was an ancient man with smaller, withered fairy wings and the right side of his body covered with iridescent crystal.

The matrons were terrified and intimidated by the sight of the three men, who each approached the women to ask for Raevyria. Auraedeus, being the Prime Crysteor, quite literally commanded them to submit the little girl into their custody. The second man offered large gold coins in exchange for Raevyria.

The third man, limping, approached the astonished matrons and greeted himself as if he was an old friend.

'Hello, my name is Demethari,' said the aged Crysteor, 'I apologise for our abrupt arrival, but I was wondering if I might have a word with this child?' The petrified matrons nodded and Raevyria, who was shyly hiding behind their skirts, timidly stepped forward. 'Hello little dear, what is your name?' Demethari asked softly.

'My name's Raevyria Blazeonheart,' said the little girl anxiously.

'Raevyria? What a beautiful name!' exclaimed Demethari as he reached his hand out to shake the little girl's, 'I'm Demethari.' Raevyria, feeling more at ease, took the old man's hand and reciprocated the gentle grip, which made Demethari chuckle. 'Awww, what a tiny hand. Raevyria, may I have a word with you about something very important?' The little girl nodded as Demethari lead Raevyria to the rocking chair beside the roaring fire and sat the little girl in it.

'Raevyria,' Demethari said seriously, 'Have you been able to see things that nobody else can't? Have you been able to do things you can't explain when you have been feeling happy or scared or angry?' Raevyria sat for a moment and thought about what the kind stranger had asked her. There were a few things she could think about. She remembered a time she saw swirls of rainbow light dance around her, but when she told one of the matrons about it, she said it was only her imagination. She also recalled a time when she was picked on by the other children for supposedly talking to a child who was, apparently, not there. She then remembered a time when she was so scared and upset of thunder and lightning, she made all the windows at the orphanage shatter. The more she thought about it, the more she could remember.

But before Raevyria could respond, a matron suddenly found some courage and shouted,

'You damn right there have been times when the little freak has been weird!' bellowed one of the matrons. Auraedeus and the winged companion glared at the matron as if she had offended them directly. Suddenly, Auraedeus conjuring a crystal wand and held it threateningly at the woman,

'You know,' hissed the Prime Crysteor through gritted teeth, 'It is people like you that makes me wonder if our sacrifice is worth your miserable life.' The matron gulped as she took a step back and shielded herself behind her whimpering colleague. Sacrifice? Raevyria did not know what the word meant, but to her it sounded scary and not a happy word. Satisfied that his point had been made, the Prime Crysteor approached Demethari and Raevyria and knelt before the little girl. 'Raevyria, my name is Auraedeus Auramaedes, and I am telling you now that you are not a freak, or weird, or strange. You are just simply, special.' The Prime Crysteor held out his hand and conjured a beautiful, iridescent butterfly. Raevyria was entranced by the spectacle she had just

6

witnessed, and both she and Demethari chuckled as the butterfly flew away from the open window. The Winged companion also smiled at the sight of the butterfly, but neither of the matrons could see the beauty the Prime Crysteor had created. 'You see, we can see and do things that nobody can do too. The reason why we can see and do such things is because we are Crysteors, and I am the Prime Crysteor. If you come with us, to Sacregard, we can teach you to harness this power and use it for a greater good.'

'Raevyria?' said Demethari softly, 'How would you like to come with us? To Sacregard? I would take very good care of you, I promise.' Tears began to well up in Raevyria's eyes as she took Demethari's offering hand and followed Prime Crysteor Auraedeus and their winged companion outside. As they made their way outside, Demethari handed Raevyria a small piece of card and as Raevyria read it she realized it was a train ticket. At that moment, an iridescent portal opened, and a beautiful opalescent steam train called *The Locomystic* appeared from the portal on enchanted tracks, blowing rainbow smoke. *The Locomystic* stopped before the group, allowing them to board the train before it disappeared into another portal and vanished into the night as they left the matrons to marvel over the gold coins they had accepted from the three Crysteors in exchange for Raevyria.

The Realm of Sacregard was an enchanting and marvelous land; surrounded by vast grasslands, enlightening forests and clear blue rivers was its majestic, nacre crystal City with buildings that towered so high into the sky that some of them even reached above the clouds. One such building, the Crystaverse, was a magnificent Castle situated in the very heart of the Sacregard. All the buildings glimmered under the morning light of the rising Sun-Turtle, Sol'Astriel, as the Moon-Turtle, Lune'Astriel, disappeared into the distance to enter its daily slumber.

The Courtyard of the Crystaverse was bustling with Crysteors of different ages and races. The humans were practicing their spellcasting with a variety of different weapons; some had wands, others had swords, and some even had long staves, while there were some who did not use a weapon at all. Also practicing their spellcasting were the Elfaery, the human-sized fairy race Demethari and his winged companion belonged to. There were also Aquara, an aquatic race of humanoid beings with rubbery skin and long tentacles for hair, who were swimming in the moat conjuring enchanted bomb-bubbles at one another.

The training of the Crysteors came to a stop when a portal appeared and *The Locomystic* stopped in the centre of the Courtyard, with Prime Crysteor himself disembarking the train with his two aides accompanied by a little human girl. The Crysteors bowed their heads to their leader and quickly began to gossip about the little human girl.

'She must be a new recruit,' whispered a human to an Elfaery,

'I wonder if she is going to be Master Demethari's new protégé?' said an Aquara to an Elfaery. The whispers and the chattering soon dispersed when the Prime Crysteor and his Elfaery Companion made their way across the Courtyard and into the Crystaverse. Demethari and Raevyria remained where they were. Noticing the Crysteors staring at her, Raevyria hid behind Demethari.

'Don't be scared,' said Demethari reassuringly as he held the little girl's hand even tighter, 'They are like you and me, they are our comrades and friends.' Raevyria peered around her new friend and observed the staring Crysteors, some gave her gentle smiles, some gave her little waves, and some gave her a respectful nod of the head. Raevyria shyly smiled and waved back as the bustling of the Crysteors training continued. Raevyria watched in awe at the power the Crysteors had, and it was beautiful.

'Mister Demethari sir? Will you teach me how to do that?' asked Raevyria hopefully. Demethari chuckled.

'That is the idea,' smiled the aged Elfaery, 'As of today you will be a pupil under my tutelage, understood?'

'Understood,' said Raevyria excitedly, 'When do we start?'

'Right now,'

Before Demethari could begin, however, a massive ball of fire descended from the skies and landed directly in the centre of the Courtyard, almost landing on the human and Elfaery Crysteors that were practicing their spellcasting. Instinctively the Crysteors summoned bubbles of water and immediately put the roaring flames out. Looking in the direction the ball of fire came from, Raevyria could see two figures sitting at the top of the Crystaverse's largest spire.

'DENAVAYDA! BELVAFREYA!' shouted Demethari angrily, 'You two get down here right now!' Raevyria watched as the two figures leapt off the top of the tower spire and glided down towards the Courtyard. The closer they came, the more Raevyria could distinguish their features. The figures turned out to be a boy and a girl, no more than twelve years of age. The boy and girl, who were twins, both had long crimson red hair fastened in braids, bright fire-blue epicanthic eyes, large pointy ears, and pale skin. The feature that attracted Raevyria the most about the twins were their crimson feathered wings. Their wings were so large they dragged on the floor behind them.

'It wasn't my fault!' said the twins in unison,

'I don't care whose fault it is.' Said Demethari firmly, 'Reckless behaviour like that will not be tolerated, even in the Crystaverse's grounds, understood?'

'Yes Master Demethari,' said the twins sullenly. Their sullenness, however, quickly changed to curiosity when they noticed Raevyria. The boy took a closer look at the little girl and sniffed her hair.

'A newbie,' said the boy with a mischievous grin, 'We're going to have a lot of fun with you. I'm Denavayda, and this is my sister, Belvafreya.' Belvafreya, the sister, also approached Raevyria and sniffed her.

'I always wanted a little sister,' said Belvafreya happily, 'Come on, let's go and have some fun!'

'Wait a moment,' said Demethari as the twins began to drag Raevyria away, 'We have only just arrived, Raevyria hasn't even been initiated yet.' The twins looked at their aged Master and sighed,

'Fine, but we'll be back for her,' said Denavayda as he and his sister let go of Raevyria, outstretched their wings, and ascended into the sky and returned to the spire they were previously perched on. Raevyria watched in amazement as the twins flew away, watching them fly made the little girl want to have wings of her own.

'I'm sorry about those two,' said Demethari sincerely, 'They are a bit boisterous, but they mean well.'

'What are they?' Raevyria asked wonderingly.

'Denavayda and Belvafreya Soulfire are Furyvires,' said Demethari, impressed by Raevyria's curiosity, 'Furyvires are a race of warriors with incredible strength and the ability to create and control fire, as they have just 'delicately' demonstrated,' Demethari and Raevyria observed the small, singed crater in the Courtyard, 'They come from the Western Realm of Valarvaal.'

'What race of people do you belong to Master Demethari?' Raevyria asked as she observed her new Master's old, withered wings.

'Me? I'm an Elfaery,' said Demethari, 'A race of peacekeepers born with the ability to manipulate the element of earth. I was born in the Northeastern Realm of Elvarorah many, many years ago and came to the Crystaverse to learn the ways of the Crysteors when I was your age.'

'And what are they?' asked Raevyria as she pointed at a group of Aquara playing in the water.

'Those are Aquara,' replied Demethari, 'As their name suggests, they are a people that can create and control water. They hail from the Eastern Realm of Aqualasia.'

'Why are all these different people here?'

'Because they are Crysteors.'

'But what *is* a Crysteor?' Demethari paused for a moment as he made the sudden realization that neither he, the Prime Crysteor nor their Elfaery Companion explained to Raevyria what a Crysteor was.

Demethari led Raevyria to a small bench on the outskirts of the Courtyard and sat down beside her.

'Crysteors are on order of beings who are born with the ability to see and control a ubiquitous power known as the Onceway,' said Demethari. Raevyria looked in puzzlement at the aged Elfaery,

'What's the Onceway?' Raevyria asked innocently,

'The Onceway is what gives a Crysteor their power,' explained Demethari, 'It is a binding, metaphysical and supernatural force that exists all around us, and as Crysteors we can use it to perform incredible feats and do extraordinary things. Do you remember the butterfly the Prime Crysteor conjured? That is the Onceway. The colourful lights you can see, that is also the Onceway. The spells those humans and Elfaery are casting over there, that is the Onceway. The Onceway itself flows through a Crysteor's veins, it is what binds the world together and our ability to see and use it is our gift, and our curse, from Ultimate Destiny.'

'Ultimate Destiny? What is that?' Raevyria asked intrigued. Demethari hesitantly paused for a moment before continuing,

'Ultimate Destiny is a conversation for when you are a little older,' said Demethari. The aged Elfaery stood up and presented his hand to Raevyria, 'But for now, we must initiate you and begin your education and training, there is no time like the present.' Raevyria took Demethari's hand and together they went inside the Crystaverse as Master and Apprentice.

Chapter Two

An Important Lesson

Demethari escorted Raevyria through the long, winding corridors of the Crystaverse until they came to the dormitories located in the highest tower. The Master and apprentice entered a room full of beds and bunk beds. Demethari pointed to a single bed located on the far side of the room.

'This will be your room, and this will be your bed,' said Demethari, 'As you can see, you'll be sharing this room, but this bed and this chest will be your responsibility, understood?' Raevyria nodded and yawned, although it was morning, she felt exhausted, after all, she did not get a wink of sleep the night before as she was journeying with the Prime Crysteor, Demethari and their winged companion onboard *The Locomystic*.

Demethari reached into his belt and, from a sheath attached to it, he pulled out a long nacre wand with a wooden handle. With a swish of the wand, he conjured a small cup which contained white liquid inside of it.

'First thing is first,' said Demethari, 'I need you to rest. This elixir will help you get the sleep you need, so when you wake up, we can begin your training.' Demethari then handed the cup to Raevyria and, without questioning it, she drank the drink in one gulp and immediately began to feel its effects. Drowsily, she stumbled towards her bed, wrapped up in a blanket and immediately fell into a deep sleep.

Raevyria did not have a dreamless sleep as she had a dream about having wings of her own and flying alongside the twins Denavayda and Belvafreya. The trio flew through the clouds, laughing and performing daring feats. In the dream Demethari was watching them, laughing happily as Raevyria, Denavayda and Belvafreya flew around the Crystaverse's towers. But suddenly, the ground around the Crystaverse began to shake and crumble. The Crystaverse collapsed into the earth and Demethari, Denavayda and Belvafreya disappeared, Raevyria found herself all alone as dark swirling shadows arose from the cracked and broken ground. Horrific black creatures rose from the destruction, hissing and snarling maniacally, followed by an even larger monster with dark purple eyes and adorned with horns and claws. The monster roared and, seeing Raevyria, it reached out one of its clawed hands to her and muttered something the little girl could not make out. Raevyria screamed as she found herself being confined in strands of black corporeal matter and pulled towards the gaping jaws of the monster, and just as the monster was about to eat her, she woke up, screaming.

Disorientated, Raevyria rose from her bed and found herself in the dormitory. The Crystaverse was still standing. Sol'Astriel was rising and the birds were chirping happily outside. Despite feeling assured it was only a dream, Raevyria felt uneasy and alone. But she was not alone, watching over her were the twins, Denavayda and Belvafreya, and they both looked concerned.

'Are you alright?' the twins asked in unison. Raevyria looked at the pair and sighed,

'Yes, I just had a bad dream,' said Raevyria,

'The first night here is always the worst,' said Belvafreya as she wrapped one of her wings around Raevyria's shoulder.

'Yeah, but it gets better, you'll see,' said Denavayda. Raevyria felt slightly reassured by Belvafreya and Denavayda's kind words. She did not know why, but she felt very safe being with the twins, even though she had only just met them. Raevyria got out of bed and felt a sharp pain in the backs of her legs, causing her to stumble and fall back on the bed.

'My legs hurt,' Raevyria winced.

'That'll go too.' Said Denavayda softly as he began rubbing the little girl's legs, 'I think it's that drink Demethari gave you.'

'I think so too,' said Belvafreya, 'All Crysteors who come here experience pain on the first night.'

'Did you two have pain when you first came here?' asked Raevyria curiously.

'No,' said the twins in unison.

'How come?' said Raevyria, growing more and more curious.

'Because we're not Crysteors,' replied the twins indifferently. Raevyria looked at the twins surprised,

'You're not Crysteors?' Raevyria asked,

'Nope, Furyvires can't be Crysteors,' Said Denavayda indifferently,

'There has never been a Furyvire Crysteor,' Belvafreya said sullenly as she rose up from the bed and stretched, 'No one knows why, but that's probably why the Crimson Guard is important.' Raevyria looked at Belvafreya baffled. Before Raevyria could ask what the Crimson Guard was, Denavayda began explaining,

'The Crimson Guard is an elite of Furyvires who work with and serve the Crysteors,' said Denavayda, 'We can serve as soldiers, protectors, advisors, whatever really.'

'Are you two members of the Crimson Guard?' asked Raevyria, intrigued.

'We're training to be,' said the twins, 'Speaking of which, we better go.' Denavayda and Belvafreya approached the large open windows of the dormitory and stretched their wings. Belvafreya leapt out of her window and glided away, while Denavayda looked back and smiled at Raevyria.

'By the way,' Denavayda said softly, 'Your new wands are in your chest and Demethari wants you to meet him in the Courtyard as soon as you are ready.'

'Okay, thank you Denavayda,' said Raevyria appreciatively. Raevyria crawled across her bed and opened the chest. Inside were two beautiful iridescent crystal wands with silver handles encrusted with gold. A swell of excitement filled Raevyria as she giggled at the sight of them. She picked them up and held them close to her chest when she realized Denavayda was happily watching her. Denavayda and Raevyria looked at one another for a moment before Denavayda leapt down from the window and approached her,

'Want to take the scenic route?' Denavayda asked. Raevyria looked at Denavayda puzzled, but before she could answer she found herself in his arms and flew out of the window. The view of Sacregard from above was breathtaking, Raevyria's dream did not do the real thing any justice. The crystal buildings illuminated in the light of Sol'Astriel, the long, winding streets bustled with so many different forms of life, and the sky was the clearest blue Raevyria had ever seen. Flying with Denavayda was all Raevyria wanted to do, she could have done this forever.

Content that he had made Raevyria all the happier, Denavayda flew down into the Crystaverse's Courtyard and gently placed her on the ground, where Demethari was waiting. Demethari, with a smile, gave Denavayda a nod, which the boy reciprocated and, with one great flap of his wings, Denavayda was back in the air. Raevyria felt a little disappointed that the flight was over, but she was glad to see Demethari.

'Good morning Raevyria,' smiled Demethari. Did you enjoy your morning flight with Denavayda?'

'I did!' said Raevyria excitedly, 'It was absolutely amazing!'

'I'm glad you enjoyed it,' chuckled Demethari, 'The twins seem to have taken a liking to you, especially Denavayda.'

'And I like them! I like them very much.'

'That is reassuring to know. One day you might need them, and they might need you.' Before Raevyria could ask what Demethari meant, the ancient Elfaery clapped his hands and a small group of Crysteors the same age as Raevyria surrounded Demethari and sat obediently on the soft grass. As soon as all the other children settled, Raevyria sat down as Demethari unsheathed his wands and began his instruction, 'Now, today we are going to be talking about our wands,' said Demethari firmly, 'Our wands are an essential part of a Crysteor's existence as they serve as an extension of ourselves. Although we can use the Onceway without them, our wands take the strain of using it for us. I highly recommend that you always use your wands, and only use the Onceway wandless unless it is necessary, understood?'

'Yes Master Demethari,' said the children together, all except Raevyria, who just nodded her head.

'Very good,' smiled the aged Elfaery, 'Now, you are probably wondering why you have two wands instead of only one? That is rather simple. One wand is for offensive Onceway and the other is for defensive. You use one wand to attack and the other to defend, although you can use both as weapons in their original forms. Allow me to demonstrate.' With a swish of one of his wands, Demethari conjured an animated training dummy and performed a variety of impressive melee attacks on the dummy as if the wands were knives. Then, with a swish of both wands, one wand turned into a sword and the other transformed into a shield. The children watched in awe as the aged Master demonstrated incredible martial feats against the training dummy.

One Crysteor, an Aquara child, raised their hand and, in a snobbish tone of voice, they asked, 'Master Demethari? Why do we need to learn how to fight?'

'Because that is our duty,' said Demethari calmly, 'We are Crysteors and it is our purpose, our destiny, to oppose any threat that befalls the world of Foreverearth and its Realms. One day, when you are old enough and trained enough, you will leave the Crystaverse to travel to these Realms and protect them from Sinscourge and the Darkaenian Supremacy.'

'What is Sinscourge?' asked an Elfaery child, not bothering to raise their hand.

'Sinscourge is a primordial, ethereal plague that has tormented the world for thousands of years,' explained Demethari, 'Sinscourge has the power to taint the mind and corrupt the hearts of those it touches. Once a being has been touched by the plague, they lose all sense of self and become merciless monsters known as the Sinscourged…but we, Crysteors, are the only ones with the power and the ability to repel the Sinscourge and fight those that have been cursed by its touch. That is why you are learning how to fight, so you can defend yourselves and protect those who do not have the power to do so.'

Demethari's sword and shield returned to their original forms and, with a swish from one of the wands, Demethari cast a barrier around himself.

'Now children, what I want you to do is cast basic attacks at me using your wands. It doesn't matter which one you choose to be your offensive wand and your defensive wand, but you need to try to break my barrier, understood? You can use the wands in their original forms or alternatively turn them into different weapons. It is your choice. Use your imagination; imagine what weapon you want your wand to turn into and the Onceway shall do the rest.'

'Yes Master Demethari,' said the children as they rose to their feet, wands in hands. Flurries of iridescent light soon shot out from the wands of most of the children, who chose to attack Demethari's barrier with the Onceway itself, but as their lights struck Demethari's barrier they were immediately deflected back at the children, knocking them off their feet and flailing through the air. The rest of the children transformed their wands into swords and shields and charged towards Demethari's barrier, only to be blasted backwards upon impact with the Oncewayankind barrier. Demethari was unfazed by his students attempts to attack him, even though they were coming at him from all directions.

Raevyria cast a bolt of light at Demethari, but when it deflected back at her, she dropped her wands and instinctively created a barrier around herself as she ducked out of its way. She suddenly felt a sharp pain in her chest that pulsated throughout her entire body. Concerned, Demethari dashed over to Raevyria's side,

'Raevyria, are you alright?' asked the aged Master worriedly. Raevyria winced as she held onto her chest and nodded. She was not sure if it was her imagination or not, but she was certain that she saw a light shine from her chest from where the pain began, but by the time Demethari came to her aid, both the light and the pain subsided. 'Using the Onceway wandless is painful, strenuous and takes years of practice that only the most powerful Crysteors can accomplish,' said Demethari, 'That is why our wands are so important, without them your Heartcrux will become exposed, and your Crysterial Progression will begin.' Raevyria looked at Demethari perplexed, as did the other children. Demethari sighed as he sat on the ground beside Raevyria. 'I'm sorry, I spoke out of turn, that is information you are not allowed to know until you are older, much older... but since I have now mentioned it, I will tell you, please sit and listen to me very carefully.' Obediently, the children sat around Demethari and listened as Demethari tentatively began to speak, 'All Crysteors, including you and me, are born with a second heart, a crystal heart known as a Heartcrux. The Heartcrux is made of pure Onceway, it flows through our veins, our very beings, and is the source of our power. However, with that power comes a price. When we have used too much of our Onceway, the Heartcrux begins to emerge from our chests and when it does that is when Crysterial Progression begins... Crysterial Progression is the name we give to the terminal illness that comes with being a Crysteor. As we continue to use the Onceway, our bodies slowly begin to turn crystal until it kills us. Crysterial Progression can, however, make you immortal as it will protect you from other illnesses, wounds from mortal weapons and even injuries that would be considered grave to others...but Crysterial Progression *will kill you*. That is why the wands are so important, they take the strain, so our bodies won't have to, allowing us to live longer to prevent the Heartcrux from emerging and to keep Crysterial Progression at bay for as long as possible...so please, no more wandless Onceway, understood?'

It was a lot to take in. The thought of dying terrified Raevyria. She looked at her aged Master and observed the crystal that covered half of his face. Was that the result of Crysterial Progression? Did that mean his Heartcrux was exposed? Raevyria wanted to ask but refrained from doing so as she noticed how distressed her Master appeared to be.

After composing himself, Demethari continued to teach the children about offensive and defensive Onceway and taught them how to create a protective barrier around themselves with their wands. It was a long and exhausting day, but Raevyria wanted to know more about Sinscourge, the Heartcrux and Crysterial Progression.

'Master Demethari?' said Raevyria, 'Pardon me for asking, but your face, is that the result of Crysterial Progression?' Demethari paused for a moment before responding,

'Yes,' sighed Demethari, 'I was very reckless in my youth, I took the power I had for granted and used it for silly, trivial things. As a result, my Heartcrux became exposed... even since then I have been vigilant and careful when using my Onceway so to prolong my life.'

'Master Demethari...I'm scared,' said Raevyria tearfully. 'I don't want to die.'

'You won't die, not for a very long time,' said Demethari reassuringly, placing his hands of Raevyria's shoulder, 'If you restrict the use of your Onceway and always use your wands then you can have a long and fulfilling life...' Demethari then appeared as if he wanted to say something else, but refrained himself from doing so. After a moment, Demethari patted Raevyria on the head and bid her good night before leaving the little girl alone in the Courtyard.

Raevyria was not on her own for long, however, as the twins Denavayda and Belvafreya arrived shortly after, attired in black leather adorned with red armour and feathers. Both had beaming smiles on their faces,

'Hi Raevyria,' said the twins happily, 'How did your first day go?'

'Great,' said Raevyria unenthusiastically, 'Do you two know about the Heartcrux and Crysterial Progression?' Denavayda and Belvafreya's happy demeanor suddenly faded into horror,

'How do you know about that?' asked a shocked Belvafreya,

'Master Demethari taught us about it today.' Raevyria replied as she sat herself on a bench and sighed sadly, 'I accidentally used the Onceway wandless, so he told us about the Heartcrux and Crysterial Progression.'

'He shouldn't have done that!' said Denavayda angrily, 'Telling little kids' stuff like that, I'm sure the old man is going senile.'

'I think he meant well,' said Belvafreya, 'If it were me, I think I'd rather know sooner than later, give me time to get my head around it.'

'I suppose,' said Raevyria sadly, 'Master Demethari did say than if I restrict my Onceway and always use my wands then I can have a fulfilling life… I want to be the greatest Crysteor I can be, but how am I supposed to defend myself without using the Onceway? How can I protect anyone without it?' Denavayda and Belvafreya smiled at each other and sat themselves beside Raevyria.

'That's where we come in,' said the twins. Raevyria looked at the twins baffled,

'What do you mean? Can you two help me?' asked Raevyria curiously,

'We've been accepted into the Crimson Guard,' smiled Belvafreya, 'Which means we'll be working together a bit more.'

'Yep, and we can officially teach you how to fight without the Onceway,' grinned Denavayda, 'So if you're serious about being the greatest Crysteor you can be we can give you some additional training.'

'Really?!' exclaimed Raevyria hopefully.

'Really,' said Belvafreya,

'Demethari and the other Masters teach about the mysticism and the use of the Onceway, the Crimson Guard teaches you how to fight without it.' said Denavayda, 'Who better teach you than us?'

'That's great! When can we begin!?' asked Raevyria earnestly,

'Right now, if you want?' said the twins.

Eagerly, Raevyria jumped up to her feet and awaited further instructions. Surprised and impressed, Denavayda and Belvafreya stood up and began their instruction. To demonstrate their prowess, the twins engaged in swift, martial arts combat. Raevyria watched in awe as Denavayda and Belvafreya fought each other. From what she observed, Denavayda was the primary attacker while

Belvafreya blocked many of his blows. Their martial arts were impressive and graceful, athletic, and almost balletic. The battle soon ended and Denavayda and Belvafreya bowed to one another. Raevyria could not help but applaud their demonstration.

'That was incredible!' beamed Raevyria, 'Please teach me!'

'Are you sure?' asked the twins seriously, 'We will be your Masters in martial arts, so you will have to treat us and respect us as such, understood?'

'Yes…Masters,' Raevyria smiled as she bowed to her new Masters, and they reciprocated the gesture.

The twins did not waste any time. They immediately began their instruction and taught Raevyria how to defend herself against basic blows and kicks with her arms and legs. Belvafreya demonstrated to Raevyria the necessary defensive poses, and Denavayda showed her how to perform basic attacks. Raevyria enjoyed learning from Denavayda and Belvafreya. It was not that she did not enjoy Demethari's lesson, but the twins had a way of learning how to fight fun and enjoyable.

Learning how to fight from Denavayda and Belvafreya became a part of Raevyria's daily routine. Every day, Raevyria would dedicate herself to learning how to fight from the twins, and other mischievous things, and continued to learn how to control her Onceway under the watchful eye of Demethari. Under

Demethari's tutelage, Raevyria studied hard and learned more about the world of Foreverearth itself and how it was made up of nine Realms: Luxdanion, Elvarorah, Aqualasia, Thaedessa, Darkaeus, Ghalatel, Valarvaal, Zorainiah and Sacregard, and one interdimensional plane of existence known as Spiritus.

Luxdanion, the Northern Realm, was the homeland of the humans and the headquarters of the Sanctuary, the most dominant religious order in the world of Foreverearth. The rulers of the Kingdoms of Luceria, Luxa, Mt. Tremmond Skai, Jenora, Havenspire, Gilderon, Oaldonathor and Respadawne were ruled by Kings and Queens known collectively as "The Council of Light". Lukiem, a small island off the northern coast of the mainland of Luxdanion where Raevyria came from, was not a domain of Luxdanion and was, in fact, under the occupation of the Emberwill Empire.

Elvarorah, the Northeastern Realm was the homeland of the Elfaery race. Elvarorah was where Foreverearth's largest forest, the World Forest, was situated and protected by an ancient order of guardians known as the Li'ay. The three largest trees in the world were where the Elfaery established their societies, also known as the "Tree Cities"; the Tree City if Amariel, the Tree City of Freyciel and the Tree City of Timerion.

Aqualasia, the Eastern Realm and the home of the aquatic Aquara, aquatic humanoid beings born with the ability to control and manipulate water. Aqualasia itself was a serene place full of towns and cities built both above and below the water. The Pool of Sorrows, The Boiling Sea of Xufeng, The Depths of Serenity and The Falls of Tranquility were the main cities of Aqualasia, under the leadership of its capital, Aqualasia City.

Thaedessa, the Southeastern Realm, was the home of a titan race of mighty and rocky Gorogorogs who lived and thrived in the mountains of Emerest and Snow Crest, the tallest Mountains in all Foreverearth. The Domains of Sledge, Blitzard, Wintersky, Glace, Yukito and Snowcrest were vast, dangerous wintery wastelands with small civilizations that surrounded the Scar, a majestic crater that was twice the size of Realm of Sacregard.

Darkaeus, the Southern Realm, known as the Realm of Corruptors, was the place where the Darkaenian Supremacy was headquartered and where it rose to power. The Realm of Darkaeus consisted of nine countries; each one ruled by a Lord Corruptor. On the main continent were the countries of Vorgause, Tenebrae, Nezdraken, Chaosii, Veildom and Warcaust which surrounded the country of Darkaenia, the seat of the Darkaenian Supremacy's power, while around the mainland were the island countries of Nearzio, Darkore and the infamous prison Cerasgrad. Darkaeus was where Sinscourge was at its strongest. The Corruptors of Darkaeus practiced and mastered the use of Sinscourge in the Land of Discord, where their creations, the Sinscourged, roamed wildly.

Ghalatel, the Southwestern Realm, was a dangerous place covered in a vast desert known as the Bravaasi Desert where the ancient, mysterious and nomadic Omenads roamed. The countries of Bhusetta, Kalamasca, Sherezbha, Arabah and Zeldin were governed by the Darshan Chiefs, who in turn served the enigmatic Darshan Sage of Bravaasi City, which was situated in the heart of the treacherous desert.

Valarvaal, the Western Realm, was the homeland of the Furyvires under the protection of the Emberwill Empire, who had an uneasy alliance with the Darkaenian Supremacy in accordance with the mysterious Shadowfire Accords. Valavaal was made up of six islands: Arazuma, Veneldin, Pyravillion, Kasai-Kaen, Fiyero and Obeliem. Arazuma was the Capital of Valarvaal and the seat of power of the Emberwill Empire and the home of House Emberwill, the Royal Family of Valarvaal, while the island of Obeliem was where the Soulfire family of Furyvires, who were known for becoming Crimson Guards and for being protectors and advisors of Crysteors, hailed from.

Zorainiah, the Northwestern Realm, was a multicultural land whose hope was to unite all the peoples of Foreverearth but became a place of unrest and civil war as everyone fought for more of Zorainiah's land. The Land of Horizon, the Tree City of Midori, the Well of Prosperity, the Ice Domain of Sickle, the land of Darken, the Imperial Province of Zakura and Starness City were the countries that made up the Realm of Zorainiah, and each one of them were desperate to become the Captial of Zorainiah. Starness City was renowned across the world of Foreverearth for being technologically advanced and superior compared to the rest of the world; they had weapons called "guns" and transportation known as "helicopters" and used these machines to keep the other countries of Zorainiah in check. Despite having these splendid weapons, transportations and other technological marvels, the President of Starness City had no resolve to conquer the rest of the world and solely wanted peace in Zorainiah.

Sacregard, the Central Realm of Foreverearth, was the Realm famous for collecting and training the most powerful Crysteors in the world and bestowing them to the other Realms to serve as protectors and warriors against the Sinscourged of the Darkaenian Supremacy.

When it came to studying the interdimensional realm known as Spiritus, Raevyria was not taught very much as very little was known about it. Spiritus was believed to be under the watchful and careful gaze of an entity known as Wraithen, the world's psychopomp and the protector of the Holylight of all living things, as well as the death of all living things.

Raevyria took her educational studies very seriously and did whatever she could to learn more, however, whenever Raevyria asked about gods, deities, and Ultimate Destiny, she was told that she would have to be a Master of the Crystaverse to learn 'Classified Information', so that became her new ambition, the become a Master of the Crystaverse and be the best Crysteor she could be.

Chapter Three

The Trials of Mastery

Six years had passed since Raevyria arrived in Sacregard, and she blossomed into a beautiful young lady. Her emerald eyes glistened, her long golden hair braided down to her waist, and her lips were as red as roses. Raevyria's natural human beauty attracted a lot of attention from the Crysteors that lived with her in the Crystaverse. The boys and men swooned over her and many of the girls and women were in awe of her looks, but no one hated her as Raevyria did not only grow up into a beauty, but she also grew up to be a kind and caring young woman; she was often the first one to greet and comfort the new Crysteors that came to the Crystaverse and was always the one who offered to help lost souls find their way through the long and confusing corridors of the Crystaverse.

Everyone in the Crystaverse cared for Raevyria, but none more so than the twins Denavayda and Belvafreya, especially Denavayda. Having grown up together for six years, Denavayda grew increasingly protective of Raevyria, especially when she started receiving unwanted attention from the boys. Belvafreya would often tease Denavayda and accuse him of being in love with Raevyria himself, but Denavayda repeatedly denied it.

The day of her fifteenth birthday was an important day for Raevyria, not because it was her birthday, but because now that she was fifteen years of age, she could take part in an even known as 'The Trials of Mastery.' Raevyria first learned about The Trials of Mastery when she was twelve years old, during an eventful lesson with Demethari and other Crysteors her age. It was eventful as Keanu Crescent's Heartcrux became exposed and he had an emotional breakdown, which was understandable. It was during this lesson that Demethari mentioned The Trials of Mastery in which a Crysteor can become a Master and be free to either leave Sacregard and travel to other Realms or stay and teach the next, small generation of Crysteors. Although she loved Sacregard and considered it her home, Raevyria wanted to travel the Realms of Foreverarth and see the world before the inevitable happened.

Demethari had asked to see Raevyria early on the morning of her fifteenth birthday, so as instructed Raevyria arose from her dreamless sleep in the early hours of the morning and crept out of the dormitory, through the long, winding corridors of the Crystaverse and into the Courtyard, where Demethari was patiently waiting for her.

'Good morning Raevyria,' whispered Demethari, 'Happy birthday,'

'Thank you Master Demethari,' Raevyria whispered back. She looked all around and noticed that the entire Courtyard was completely deserted. It was the first time she had ever seen it so empty before. 'Master? Why are we up so early?'

'To begin the Trials of Mastery,' replied Demethari. Raevyria looked surprised, 'You still want to proceed with the Trials do you not?'

'Yes, yes I do.' Said Raevyria eagerly,

'Excellent,' beamed Demethari, 'Now remember, these Trials are to test your wisdom, power, and courage. You may find them either ridiculously easy or frustratingly difficult. The Trials are different for each person. Now, for the first Trial, you are to be tested on your wisdom to tame your very own Starbird.'

Raevyria's eyes lit up, she had always wanted her own Starbird ever since she encountered her first one when she was twelve years old. Starbirds were large, majestic creatures that resembled a four-legged eagle with large antlers, three pairs of wings and long feathered tails with either gold, white, black, brown, or grey plumage. The Starbird Raevyria encountered years ago was a Starbird called Dawnfire, she was an easy going Starbird with a gentle temperament, but that was only because she had been trained and raised by Crysteors. If Raevyria was to tame her own Starbird, she imagined it would not be an easy feat, considering it was one of the tests in the Trials of Mastery.

Demethari escorted Raevyria just to the outskirts of Sacregard City, where many Starbirds were feasting on the corpse of a giant oxen beast. Raevyria suddenly felt uneasy,

'Now listen carefully,' said Demethari firmly, 'All you need to do is remember your training and your education and you will be able to pass the Trials. Everything I and the twins have taught you has been for this purpose.' Raevyria looked at Demethari surprised,

'You know about my training with Denavayda and Belvafreya?' asked Raevyria, bewildered.

'Of course, I do,' said Demethari, 'What kind of Master would I be if I didn't? Now go!' Demethari suddenly pushed Raevyria towards the herd of Starbirds and noticed that the entirety of the herd was watching her. A few of the Starbirds darted away from the oxen corpse, while the largest of the Starbirds charged towards Raevyria. Instinctively, Raevyria unsheathed her wands and shouted 'Protectum!', creating a barrier around herself just in time to deflect the charging Starbird. This seemed to anger the black Starbird as the Starbird reared up and attempted to claw at Raevyria, but the barrier did its job and protected her from its mighty talons. Huffing, the giant Starbird circled around Raevyria and, seeing its attempts to kill the girl were futile while the barrier was cast, the Starbird returned to devouring the oxen corpse, as did the other Starbirds.

Raevyria cautiously approached the herd, her wands in hands, and caught sight of a smaller, white Starbird that was feeding off the other side of the oxen carcass. Raevyria wanted to avoid the giant Starbird at all costs, he was not in the mood to be captured and tamed, and settled on the smaller, white Starbird.

But how was she to tame it? Raevyria recalled reading about Starbirds and remembered that they were very proud and noble creatures, as well as very intelligent. Raevyria then realized that she had been approaching the Starbirds incorrectly and immediately knew what to do. With one wand she dispelled the barrier she had created around herself, while with the other she shot a bolt of light into the air, getting the attention of the Starbirds, particularly the giant one that had attempted to kill her. As the herd of Starbirds fled and took flight, the giant, black Starbird remained behind and once again charged at Raevyria angrily. Raevyria did not run, did not attempt to hide, or protect herself and did not show any signs of fear, instead, she sheathed her wands and bowed, all the while maintaining eye contact with the Starbird. The black Starbird came to a sudden halt and observed the girl's gesture. Raevyria then lowered her head, severing the eye contact she had maintained, and bowed down even further. The Starbird was, at first, perplexed by Raevyria's actions. After a few moments, the Starbird cautiously approached Raevyria and sniffed the top of her head. Raevyria could feel its warm breath and could smell the oxen blood. She then, very slowly, raised her head and found herself looking directly into the eyes of the black Starbird, who had bowed its head down to her level, returning the gesture of respect. Raevyria held her hand out to the Starbird and the Starbird pressed its head against it, allowing Raevyria to stroke it.

Demethari's nerves were on edge. One minute he was terrified, another he was relieved but finally he was proud. Demethari watched in awe as Raevyria tamed the large black Starbird.

'Well done,' said Demethari, 'You have passed the first Trial.'

'Thank you, Master.' Raevyria smiled as the black Starbird nuzzled its large head onto her chest.

'What are you going to call him?' Demethari asked curiously. Raevyria, who did not have any idea that the Starbird was a male, stood and thought for a moment.

'I think I'll name him Scorch,' said Raevyria as she continued to stroke her new Starbird.

'Scorch? Interesting name,' mused Demethari, 'Well, now you have tamed Scorch he should let you ride him now.' Raevyria looked at Demethari anxiously,

'What?' she said hesitantly, after all, it had only been a few minutes since Scorch tried to kill her and now, she was expected to ride him. She was not sure if that was such a good idea.

'Don't worry,' said Demethari reassuringly, 'Once you have earned a Starbird's respect they will be loyal to you for the rest of their lives. That is why for generations the Starbird has been the steed of all Crysteors.' Although

Raevyria was uneasy about riding Scorch, she trusted her Master. Steadily, Raevyria patted Scorch's side and approached his back. Sensing what she was going to do, Scorch knelt and laid himself on the ground, allowing Raevyria to mount him. Raevyria climbed onto Scorch's massive back and once she was on, Scorch rose to his feet and began charging. 'I'll meet you back at the Crystaverse!' Demethari shouted as Scorch charged past him with Raevyria holding on for dear life. With a mighty flap of his wings, Scorch was soaring up into the air towards the starry skies and the colourful City of Sacregard.

Raevyria had never seen the view of Sacregard from above at night before, as Denavayda and Belvafreya were forbidden from flying at nighttime. The view was breathtaking. Raevyria had always wanted to have wings of her own, and now she finally had wings, six of them to be exact, and she loved Scorch for them. Scorch chirped happily as Raevyria softly stroked him. Scorch really was an intelligent Starbird as he immediately took Raevyria back to the Crystaverse Courtyard when Raevyria directed him to do so. Demethari watched as Raevyria and Scorch descended from the skies and landed in the Courtyard.

'Well done, Raevyria, and well done, Scorch,' said Demethari proudly. Raevyria jumped down from the Starbird's back, escorted him to the stables and placed him in an empty stall. Scorch was the tallest and most muscular of the Starbirds in the stables, and that made Raevyria feel proud of not only herself, but of Scorch too. Raevyria made sure that Scorch was comfortable and settled before she left him and returned to Demethari. 'Now then,' said Demethari calmly, 'Are you ready for the second Trial?'

'Yes Master Demethari,' said Raevyria, 'I am ready.'

Demethari reached out and took Raevyria's hand into his own then, with a swish of his wand, the pair found themselves in a beautiful emerald, green forest. Raevyria had never seen a forest like it before.

'Where are we?' asked Raevyria, who was in awe of her surroundings.

'We are in the World Forest of Elvarorah,' said Demethari, 'This is the location of your second Trial.'

'What do I need to do?' asked Raevyria curiously.

'There is a Wood Dragon that has been corrupted by Sinscourge somewhere in the World Forest,' said Demethari, 'Your Trial is to track the poor creature and deal with it accordingly.'

'You mean kill it or cure it?' asked Raevyria hesitantly,

'That is your decision to make,' replied Demethari, 'Now, begin.'

Raevyria paused for a moment as she examined her surroundings. The World Forest was indeed breathtaking but as its name implied, it was the largest forest in all Foreverearth so if she needed to track down a Sinscourged Wood Dragon in the World Forest, she would need to look for clues, or else she would be looking for it forever. Looking around, Raevyria noticed that some of the branches in the treetops were broken and covered in black ooze. It was coagulated Sinscourge. Raevyria examined the trees and noticed that there were more trees that were damaged and covered in Sinscourge. Unsheathing one of her wands, Raevyria conjured a glass jar and contained the coagulated Sinscourge she had found in it. If she had left Sinscourge where it was, it could have corrupted anyone and anything that came by. By containing the Sinscourge she found in the jar, Raevyria prevented that from happening. Raevyria followed the trail of broken trees deeper into the World Forest. As she followed the trail, she came across the torn corpse of a deer covered in blood and Sinscourge. Raevyria contained the Sinscourge in her glass jar when she suddenly heard the distressed roar of the Wood Dragon in the distance. Before she went towards the sound of the roar she checked if the trail of destruction led in the direction of the Wood Dragon. It did. Raevyria raced through the World Forest, collecting the coagulated Sinscourged as she swiftly moved through the trees, and finally came across her target.

The Wood Dragon was covered in blood and black ooze that dripped from its gaping jaws. The creature's eyes were black with corruption from the Sinscourge that had plagued its body and its mind. Raevyria now had a choice to make, to cure the Sinscourge and liberate the Wood Dragon or kill the creature and put it out of its suffering. Raevyria placed the glass jar containing the Sinscourge she had collected on the ground and unsheathed her other wand.

The Wood Dragon leapt into the air and flew past Raevyria, destroying and

tainting more trees as it went through the World Forest. With one of her wands,

Raevyria conjured an iridescent lasso and threw it around the Wood Dragon's

neck. Raevyria pulled the lasso as hard as she could, trying her best to rein in

the Wood Dragon towards her. The Wood Dragon instead pulled on the lasso

which caused Raevyria to fly towards the Wood Dragon and landed forcefully

onto its back. Raevyria held on for dear life as the Wood Dragon roared angrily,

flying, and crashing through the trees to rid itself of its unwanted rider.

Raevyria climbed up to Wood Dragon's long neck and held onto its horned

head tightly with one hand while holding a wand in the other. With the wand

pressed against the Wood Dragon's head, she began muttering the incantation,

'Reject the Sinscourge, purge the plague,' repeatedly. As she said the words

repeatedly, the painful roars of the Wood Dragon lesson as Raevyria extracted

the Sinscourge from the Wood Dragon through its eyes. The ethereal

Sinscourge dangled at the end of Raevyria's wand.

As the Wood Dragon crashed into the ground, Raevyria dispelled the lasso

and summoned the glass jar of Sinscourge to her and contained the Sinscourge

that dangled from her wand into the jar. Panting, Raevyria collapsed onto the

ground, holding the jar of Sinscourge in her hand, and looked over to the Wood

Dragon. It was not breathing, it was motionless, it was dead. But how? The Sinscourge was extracted. Demethari appeared and sighed,

'What a shame,' said Demethari sadly, 'Such a waste of a beautiful creature.'

'But Master Demethari, I don't understand,' said Raevyria, visibly upset, 'I extracted the Sinscourge, why did it die?'

'It was too tainted beyond extraction,' said Demethari, 'Sometimes, when Sinscourge is too great, extracting it can cause more harm than good. Although your intention was a noble one Raevyria, by putting it through the extraction process, you unwittingly caused it more pain. Sometimes the most merciful thing to do is to put it out of its misery.'

'Does that mean I failed?' asked Raevyria, tears streaming down her face.

'No, my dear, you passed,' smiled Demethari, 'You tracked the Wood Dragon down and contained the Sinscourge, preventing it from hurting anyone else. Although the Wood Dragon perished, you learned from this experience. Come, let's return to Sacregard for the final Trial.' Demethari once again took Raevyria's hand into his own and with a swish of his wand, they disappeared from the Wood Forest and returned to Sacregard.

When Demethari and Raevyria arrived in the Crystaverse's courtyard, they found Denavayda and Keanu sitting at a circular table with three goblets on top of it.

'Denavayda? Keanu? What are you two doing here?' asked Raevyria perplexed,

'Denavayda and Keanu are part of the final Trial,' said Demethari as he gestured to the empty seat, 'Please sit.' Uneasy, Raevyria sat at the table and looked at Denavayda and Keanu concerned. 'Raevyria Blazeonheart, you demonstrated your courage by taming the King of the Starbird herd. You demonstrated your power by confronting the Wood Dragon, and now, you must demonstrate your wisdom.' With a swish of his wand, Demethari conjured black liquid in each of the three goblets on the table and placed one goblet in front of Denavayda, the other in front of Keanu and the final one in front of Raevyria. 'One of the goblets contains a harmless liquid, the other two contain poison. Each of you can only drink from a single goblet and all the contents must be drunk. Now, begin.'

Raevyria, Denavayda and Keanu looked at each other horrified.

'Okay, let me think about this for a second,' said Raevyria nervously. 'Two goblets are poisoned, one is not. Who is most likely to have the poisoned goblets?'

'I think you and I have the poisoned goblets,' said Keanu thoughtfully,

'What makes you think that?' asked Raevyria curiously.

'Isn't it obvious?' asked Keanu, 'We're Crysteors. The worst that will happen is you'll die and be revived by your Heartcrux becoming exposed and I'm already temporarily immortal through my Crysterial Progression.'

'But won't drinking the poison cause your Crysterial Progression to progress?' asked Raevyria, 'That'll just cause you more pain, no, I'm not having that.'

'I think you're both over thinking this.' added Denavayda, 'Maybe that is what the Trial wants you to think. I think you two having the poisoned goblets is too obvious.'

'Denavayda's right,' said Raevyria seriously, 'And what if it turns out Denavayda's goblet is poisoned?'

'Why don't I just take a sip out of each goblet?' asked Keanu,

'You can't, the rules say we're only allowed to drink from a single goblet and all the contents must be drunk,' said Raevyria.

'If you think I'm going to let you risk your Heartcrux becoming exposed you can think again,' said Denavayda, 'I'd rather drink the poison than you go through that.'

'And do you think I'm going to let you risk your life for mine? I don't think so.' Raevyria argued back.

'Well then, what do you suggest?' asked Keanu. Raevyria sat and thought for what felt like a long time. She looked at the goblets and noticed something odd – none of the cups were entirely full.

'I've got it!' exclaimed Raevyria, 'Let's pour all the contents into a single goblet then that way we'll be drinking from a single goblet and be certain that it's poisoned.'

'You're a genius,' said Denavayda as he quickly began to pour the contents of the other two goblets into his own.

'What are you doing?' Keanu asked Denavayda,

'Bottoms up!' cheered Denavayda as he reached for the poisoned goblet and began to down the drink. But nothing was going in. Denavayda observed the goblet and found that Raevyria had used her wand to teleport the contents out of Denavayda's goblet and into hers. Before Denavayda and Keanu could object, Raevyria had drunk the poisoned liquid. 'What have you done?' gasped Denavayda, horrified.

'It's okay,' said Raevyria reassuringly, 'As Keanu said…I'll just be revived by my…Heartcrux…it's okay…' Raevyria slipped off her chair and collapsed on the ground. The last thing she heard was Denavayda screaming her name.

Chapter Four

The Battle Above Sacregard

The grounds around the Crystaverse began to shake and crumble as Raevyria found herself all alone as dark swirling shadows arose from the cracked and broken ground. Horrific black creatures rose from the destruction, hissing and snarling maniacally, followed by an even larger monster with dark purple eyes and adorned with horns and claws. The monster roared and, seeing Raevyria, it reached out one of its clawed hands to her and muttered something Raevyria could not make out. Raevyria screamed as she found herself being pulled towards the gaping jaws of the monster, and just as the monster was about to eat her, Raevyria woke up and found herself in her own bed, surrounded by Crysteors each holding a present and a card.

'Happy birthday!' cheered the Crysteors. Raevyria looked at them confused,

'What happened?' asked Raevyria as she observed the Crysteors and saw Keanu sitting beside her. 'Keanu? What happened?'

'You drank all the contents from a single goblet and passed the final Trial,' smiled Keanu. Raevyria suddenly looked down at her chest and noticed that her Heartcrux was not exposed, which confused her even more. 'It turns out it was just a sleeping draught that you drank, not poison,' added Keanu, 'Demethari wanted me to tell you that you passed all three Trials of Mastery and will be an official Master within a few days.' The Crysteors in the dormitory cheered as they threw Raevyria's cards and presents on her bed.

'Thank you so much,' said Raevyria, her eyes streaming with tears as she looked at the cards and the gifts, 'Really, you didn't have to go through all this trouble for me.'

'No trouble at all,' said Myles Amariel, who was an Elfaery Crysteor a couple of years younger than Raevyria.

'Denavayda and Belvafreya have gone to get the cake,' said Sparks Sinclaire, a human Crysteor the same age as Raevyria.

'Sparks, shush!' exclaimed several Crysteors as they shot him piercing glares. Raevyria laughed,

'You are all so thoughtful, thank you,' laughed Raevyria wholeheartedly. Suddenly, Denavayda and Belvafreya arrived through the window holding a poorly made cake with fifteen candles atop it.

'Happy birthday!' said the twins and, with a snap of his fingers, Denavayda lit the candles on the cake.

'Is that supposed to be a cake? It's hideous!' said Questo Aquadella, an Aquara Crysteor. Denavayda and Belvafreya looked angrily at Questo,

'Oh really!?' said Belvafreya, obviously hurt and offended by Questo's critique, 'Well maybe YOU should bake the cake next time!' But before

Belvafreya could throw it at Questo's face, Denavayda liberated the cake from Belvafreya's fury and gently placed it on Raevyria's lap.

'Happy birthday Raevyria.' Said Denavayda softly as he brushed a lock of golden hair from Raevyria's face, which caused her to blush.

'Thank you Denavayda, Belvafreya, everyone,' said Raevyria sweetly as she held the cake in her hands and blew the candles out.

"Wait, you're supposed to make a wish!' shouted several Crysteors at once.

'I don't need wishes,' smiled Raevyria as she placed the cake on her bedside table and looked at Denavayda, 'I already have everything I need.'

'I think I'm going to be sick,' groaned Belvafreya as she observed the glance between Denavayda and Raevyria and approached the window, 'Save some cake for me' Belvafreya added as she leapt out of the window and flew away.

As Raevyria got up to get changed, Denavayda ushered the Crysteors out of the dormitory to give her some privacy. Denavayda closed the door after the Crysteors and stood with his back to Raevyria.

'So… you passed the Trials of Mastery, what are you going to do now?' asked Denavayda curiously.

'I want to travel,' said Raevyria excitedly, 'I don't want our years of training to be for naught. You and Belvafreya have helped me so much, and besides, I don't want to remain in Sacregard forever, I want to go out and see the world…with you.'

'With me?' asked Denavayda, surprised. Suddenly embarrassed at the realization of what she had just said, Raevyria quickly fastened her laces and approached the door where Denavayda was standing. As Raevyria came closer, Denavayda spun round and planted a kiss on Raevyria's forehead. His lips, his touch, was so warm and gentle it made her hearts flutter and have butterflies in her stomach. Denavayda bowed his head and pressed his forehead against hers, 'You are such a sweetheart,' whispered Denavayda softly. Raevyria felt her hearts beat faster, faster than they ever have, 'Thank you, Raevyria, please don't ever change.' Before she could ask what he meant by that, Denavayda picked her up and carried her towards the window, 'Want to take the scenic route, for old times' sake?' Denavayda asked. With a nod of her head, Raevyria wrapped her arms around Denavayda's neck and together they were out of the window.

The scenic route always made Raevyria's hearts soar, she loved flying with Denavayda. He had a way of making her feel safe constantly, even when he was performing reckless stunts and maneuvers, she felt safe with him. Denavayda zigzagged and looped through the clouds high above the city of Sacregard.

The peacefulness of the scenic flight did not last for long when, suddenly, a black galleon airship penetrated the clouds and roared passed Raevyria and

Denavayda, narrowly missing them. Gathered on the deck of the airship were a horde of monstrous winged creatures with gaping jaws that dripped black ooze.

'What are they!?' gasped Raevyria, horrified at the sight of the creatures,

'They're Sinscourged,' said Denavayda, 'And that's a Darkaenian Supremacy Battleship, I've never seen them get this close to Sacregard before.' The Sinscourged, Raevyria had been training for the last six years to fight these creatures, but she had never seen them before, 'We need to report this to the Masters and the Prime Crysteor,' said Denavayda sternly as he tightened his grip on Raevyria and swooped downward towards Sacregard at incredible speed. It was the fastest Raevyria had even seen Denavayda fly before. The pair landed in the Courtyard, where a small group of new Crysteors were training, and raced into the Crystaverse.

The Masters and the Prime Crysteor, Auraedeus Auramaedes, were gathered in the Council Chamber, discussing the progress of the new Crysteors, when Raevyria and Denavayda came bursting in. The Crimson Guard immediately halted them as they entered the Chamber as the Masters gasped in surprise at the intrusion, all except Demethari and Auraedeus, who looked serious and reserved.

'What is the meaning of this?' demanded Auraedeus as both Raevyria and Denavayda were reprimanded by the Crimson Guard,

'We just saw a Darkaenian Airship, directly above Sacregard,' panted Denavayda,

'Yes, and it was occupied by Sinscourged,' added Raevyria, who was also panting. Panic chatter filled the room as Demethari and Auraedeus exchanged concerned looks,

'The Darkaenian Supremacy have never gotten this close to Sacregard before,' said Auraedeus firmly, 'They are getting bolder, I will give them that.'

'What are your orders Prime Crysteor?' asked Demethari. The Prime Crysteor paused for a moment before rising from his seat and addressing the room,

'I want the Crimson Guard to gather all Crysteors and escort them to the Courtyard and prepare them for battle as hastily as possible,' said Auraedeus. Not wasting anymore time, the Crimson Guards, accompanied by Denavayda, left the Council Chamber shouting orders in the Red Word language, 'Meanwhile,' continued Auraedeus, 'I want all Masters to go to the Gate Chamber immediately.' The Gate Chamber? In the six years Raevyria had lived in Sacregard not once had she heard about the Gate Chamber. Obeying their leader's orders, the Council Members waved their wands and teleported out of the Council Chamber. As Raevyria was about to follow the Masters when Demethari grabbed hold of her hand and pulled her to the side.

'Raevyria, this is it now,' said Demethari solemnly, 'This is your first real battle against the Darkaenian Supremacy. You are not an official Master yet, so I need you to go to the Courtyard and follow the Prime Crysteor's instructions. Remember your training and you'll be fine, also, always use your wands, no wandless Onceway, understood?'

'Understood, Master Demethari,' said Raevyria anxiously. 'But Master Demethari, what is the Gate Chamber?' Demethari took Raevyria's hands into his own and smiled,

'I will explain everything once you are officially a Master,' said Demethari reassuringly, 'But for now go to the Courtyard. You'll be fine, I believe in you.' Feeling a little braver, Raevyria nodded as Demethari teleported away and she went to Courtyard as ordered.

By the time Raevyria arrived in the Courtyard all the Crysteors were gathered around the Prime Crysteor. The younger Crysteors were anxious and afraid, while the older Crysteors were prepared and ready for combat. High in the clouds above Sacregard, Raevyria could see the shadow of the Darkaenian Battleship and the Furyvires of the Crimson Guard engaged in aerial combat with the winged creatures. From a distance, Raevyria could see Denavayda and Belvafreya using their pyromancy and sword fighting prowess to keep the creatures at bay alongside their comrades.

'Everybody, listen!' shouted Auraedeus, 'I want all Crysteors over the age of sixteen to mount their Starbirds and engage the enemy, all those under the age of sixteen are to remain here and focus on creating a barrier around Sacregard, understood?!'

'Understood,' replied the Crysteors as they began to rush around to their designated positions. The older Crysteors raced to their stables and mounted their Starbirds while the younger Crysteors began chanting 'Protectum' to create a barrier around Sacregard.

Raevyria felt torn; she wanted to help but she wanted to do more than simply cast a barrier around Sacregard. While everyone was bustling around to their positions, Raevyria snuck into the stables and approached Scorch. Raevyria gently saddled the Starbird up, rode him out of the stables and, with a gentle tug of the reins, Scorch went faster and faster and, with a mighty flap of his wings, he was up in the air and flying towards the Darkaenian Battleship.

The skies above Sacregard became a bloody battlefield and a paroxysm of light, fire, and darkness as the Crysteors and the Furyvires of the Crimson Guard clashed with the Sinscourged of the Darkaenian Supremacy. Bodies fell from both sides of the battle and dissolved in the barrier that surrounded Sacregard. Raevyria, astride Scorch, flew to Denavayda, who was fighting numerous Sinscourged alongside Belvafreya on the deck of the Darkaenian Battleship. Scorch landed on the deck and began snapping and clawing at several Sinscourged as Raevyria, with her wands at the ready, dismounted and assisted Denavayda and Belvafreya in the fight. Denavayda fought the Sinscourged with his two katana swords, Tongue, and Tooth, named so as the blade of Tongue was red and the blade of Tooth was white, while Belvafreya fought with her nodachi blade Songstress, named so as the blade 'sings' when swung.

As the trio of friends were fighting the Sinscourged, they failed to notice the appearance of a tall, Darkaenian warrior dressed from head to toe in black and purple dragonesque armour. The Darkaenian warrior silently observed Raevyria, Denavayda and Belvafreya as they used their abilities and their powers to fight the Sinscourged. With a snap of his fingers, the Darkaenian warrior summoned an ebony claymore sword in a puff of black smoke and approached the Crysteor and the two Furyvires. Belvafreya, who had just incinerated a Sinscourged with her pyromancy, noticed the approaching warrior and engaged in an epic swordfight with him while Denavayda and Raevyria were distracted by more Sinscourged. After dispatching several Sinscourged, Denavayda and Raevyria turned around to find Belvafreya impaled by the Darkaenian warrior's claymore blade.

'BELVAFREYA!' screamed Denavayda and Raevyria, horrified. Nonchalantly, the Darkaenian warrior drew his sword from Belvafreya's torso, grabbed hold of her neck and with a fierce swing of his blade he severed

Belvafreya's beautiful wings and threw her off the ship. Angered and traumatized, Denavayda could feel his blood boiling and tears stinging his eyes. In his rage, Denavayda's eyes began to glow a piercing blue as crimson flames engulfted his body. Without hesitation, he conjured and threw balls of fire toward the Darkaenian warrior. Unfazed by Denavayda's power and grief, the Darkaenian warrior simply swung his blades at the approaching fireballs and sliced through them as if they were nothing. With Tongue and Tooth in hands, Denavayda charged towards the Darkaenian warrior and engaged in battle with him. Sparks flew off the blades of both Denavayda and the Darkaenian warrior's swords. Terrified for Denavayda's safety, Raevyria cast Protectum around her beloved friend, just barely saving his life from a fatal blow to the neck. With a wave of his hand, the Darkaenian warrior summoned an ethereal stream of Sinscourge from his body and coiled it around the barrier that was protecting Denavayda and instantly destroyed it. The streams of Sinscourge bound themselves around Denavayda's limbs and neck and began to pull viciously, which caused Denavayda to suffocate and lose consciousness.

'STOP IT!' screamed Raevyria as she aimed her wands at the Darkaenian warrior and began to fire blasts of Onceway at him, which the Darkaenian warrior blocked with a wave of his other hand and conjured a Sinscourge sphere around himself. Raevyria roared in anger as the Darkaenian warrior deflected all her attack spells. 'FIGHT ME! YOU COWARD!' Raevyria shouted with tears streaming down her face as she redirected her attacks from the Darkaenian warrior to the Sinscourge that was pulling on the unconscious Denavayda's limbs. Raevyria managed to free Denavayda from the hold of Sinscourge but found herself bound instead.

The Darkaenian warrior grabbed hold of the unconscious Denavayda and threw him overboard. Tears fell from Raevyria's cheeks, her heart broken. The tall Darkaenian warrior forcefully grabbed Raevyria's chin and forced her to look into the cold eyes of his helmet. Although she could not see his eyes, she could feel them examining her. As the Darkaenian warrior looked at Raevyria, she began to hear footsteps.

'Alright brother, that will do,' said a voice from the direction of the heavy footsteps. The Darkaenian warrior stepped aside and a human in his early twenties appeared. The young man had black oily eyes, long black hair, and deathly grey skin. He was attired in the same dragonesque armour as his brother, minus the sinister helmet. He was accompanied by a skeletal Jester with the same grey skin and black eyes as his Master,

'Get away from me!' screamed Raevyria as the man and his Jester approached her.

'Very lively, aren't we?' said the armoured man as he grabbed hold of Raevyria's chin and forced her to look at him, just as his brother did, 'What's your name?' asked the man curiously. In her grief and anger, Raevyria refused

56

to respond. 'I will tell you my name, if you tell me yours?' Raevyria still refused, but her anger and grief subsided into shock and alarm when the Jester stepped forward and responded for her,

'Her name is Raevyria Blazeonheart, Prince Xeropheers,' said the Jester with a raspy voice, 'She is fifteen years old and…she has just passed her Trials of Mastery. She may be useful to us.'

'I will never help you!' screamed Raevyria angrily. As Xeropheers raised a hand to strike her, Keanu and several other Crysteors appeared on the deck of the ship and surrounded Raevyria, the Jester, Xeropheers and his brother, the Darkaenian warrior.

'Release her!' demanded Keanu. Xeropheers and his Jester laughed,

'*"Release her"*,' said the Jester mockingly. 'Little Keanu Crescent and all his little friends think they're brave.' Keanu and his Crysteor comrades looked shocked as the Jester mocked them.

'That's enough, Jester,' said Xeropheers, amused, 'It appears as though the preternatural warriors of this generation are ignorant to the power of the Corruptors and the Darkaenian Supremacy. Brother, why don't you demonstrate our might?' Without a second thought or a moment of objection, the Darkaenian warrior summoned a mist of Sinscourge from himself and sent it towards Keanu and the Crysteors that came to Raevyria's rescue and coiled itself around them.

Raevyria could hear bones crunching and muscles popping as the Sinscourge pulled on the limbs of its Crysteor captives. With another wave of his hand, the Darkaenian warrior made the Sinscourge throw the Crysteors overboard. The mist returned to the Darkaenian warrior's armour.

'What a pathetic excuse for Crysteors,' laughed Xeropheers. He then turned his attention back to Raevyria. 'Now then, what are we to do with you?'

'You might as well kill me now,' hissed Raevyria, 'I will not help you.'

'Very well,' said Xeropheers nonchalantly, and before Raevyria knew it, the Darkaenian warrior broke her neck, and everything went black.

Chapter Five

The Prisoner of Cerasgrad

The ruler of the Southern Realm of Darkaeus and the Supreme Corruptor of the Darkaenian Supremacy, Mortipher Darkaenian, was a careless, cunning, and cruel man who had a passion of inflicting pain onto others. In fact, he was in the middle of torturing his latest victim when an emissary informed him that his sons had returned from Sacregard.

'Assemble the Senate of Lord Corruptors at once,' said the Supreme Corruptor coldly and instantly the emissary departed to carry out the order.

In the centre of the Land of Discord was the Capital City of Darkaenia. Darkaenia was a vast City full of tall ebony buildings with airships and aircars dashing through its skies. In the very heart of the city was the Darkaenian Palace, the home and seat of power for the Darkaenian Family of Corruptors. This was where the Supreme Corruptor gathered the Senate of Lord Corruptors.

'Your Majesty, Supreme Corruptor Mortipher, what is the meaning of this meeting?' asked one of the Lord Corruptors curiously.

'Which one of you did it!?' hissed the Supreme Corruptor. The Lords of the Senate exchanged perplexed looks at one another, 'Which one of you gave my sons the order to go to Sacregard?'

'This is news to us,' said another Lord Corruptor, 'If I recall correctly, during our last meeting, you expressed concerns about your son, Prince Xeropheers, and his ambition.'

'And it appears my concerns were warranted,' replied Mortipher, 'My sons have the audacity to disobey my orders and venture off to Sacregard without my permission. This shall not go unpunished.' Just as another Lord Corruptor was about to contribute his opinion, Xeropheers burst through the doors and appeared before his father and the Senate of Lord Corruptors.

'Good evening father and Lord Corruptors of the Senate,' said Xeropheers nonchalantly, 'I bring exciting news.'

'Does this have anything to do with your little trip to Sacregard?' asked Mortipher angrily.

'It does,' said Xeropheers indifferently. Before Xeropheers could say anything else, Mortipher teleported to Xeropheers in a puff of black smoke and struck him.

'You *dare* disobey *me*!?' bellowed Mortipher, 'How dare you!? I gave you and your brother orders not to go to Sacregard, you could have been killed!'

'You needn't worry, Father,' Xeropheers said indifferently, 'Myself and your precious Heir are fine.'

'You exploited your brother's powers for your own interests,' hissed Mortipher.

'*Half*-brother,' said Xeropheers matter-of-factly, 'And yes I did.'

'And I presume you took the Jester with you?' growled Mortipher.

'Of course, I wouldn't have been able to get what I wanted without the Jester and your precious Heir,' said Xeropheers.

'And what is it you wanted?' asked one of the Lord Corruptors curiously. Xeropheers paused for a moment before responding,

'A Crysteor, and the wings of a Crimson Furyvire,' said Xeropheers casually. The Lord Corruptors began to chat amongst themselves anxiously, while rage consumed the Supreme Corruptor,

'You dare to bring a Crysteor here?!' asked Mortipher angrily,

'Of course not, I have sent her to Cerasgrad,' replied Xeropheers, 'I reckon she will be quite comfortable there.' The chattering amongst the Lord Corruptors became more intense, and the Supreme Corruptor stared coldly at his sneering son.

The Prison of Cerasgrad was a fortified castle on a small island southeast of the Southern Realm of Darkaeus, under the occupation of the Darkaenian

Supremacy. It was a frightening and dismal place, surrounded by a perpetual storm of thunder, lightning and heavy rain. The prison itself was full of all kinds of inmates, driven mad by the torture and the suffering they endured by the hands of the sadistic guards.

When Raevyria came to, she found herself in a small, damp, cold cell with blankets in the far corner and chains dangling down from the ceiling. The only light she had was the light from the Moon-Turtle Lune'Astriel shining through the bars of the tiny window. She also noticed she was now wearing a plain white dress which revealed her now-exposed Heartcrux. Devastated at her surroundings and remembering what had happened to her friends Denavayda and Belvafreya, Raevyria curled herself up on the floor and sobbed uncontrollably.

Raevyria sobbed for what felt like hours when she soon heard a calm and assuring voice speak to her,

'Hello? Are you okay?' asked the gentle voice. Raevyria sat up, wiping away her tears, and approached the opposite wall where the voice was coming from.

'Hello?' Raevyria sniffed as she pressed her head against the wall.

'Hello!' replied the voice cheerfully, 'Are you okay?'

'I don't know,' said Raevyria as she began to cry again, 'Where am I?'

'You're in Cerasgrad Prison,' said the voice calmly, 'It's a fortress belonging to the Supreme Corruptor and his family.'

'The Supreme Corruptor?' asked Raevyria, bewildered,

'Yes,' replied the voice, 'This is where they put their, um, how do I put this delicately? It's a place where they put their failures, as well as the prizes.'

'I don't understand,' said Raevyria,

'Don't worry about it,' said the voice softly, 'You must be the Crysteor I heard the guards talk about. What's your name?'

'Raevyria,' replied Raevyria, 'Raevyria Blazeonheart.'

'Blazeonheart?' said the voice, shocked. The voice's reaction to her name confused Raevyria.

'Is something wrong?' asked Raevyria worriedly,

'No…nothing is wrong.' Said the voice hesitantly. After a few awkward minutes of silence, the voice spoke again, 'I'm Zelderaph.'

'Zelderaph,' said Raevyria as she stroked the wall the voice came from, 'Thank you for your kindness.'

'No need to thank me,' said Zelderaph.

Suddenly and unexpectedly, Raevyria heard the unlocking of her cell door and from the door appeared three guards clad in black leather.

'See? Didn't I tell you she was a looker?' sniggered one of the guards,

'You sure did,' agreed the other two guards. Before she knew it, Raevyria found herself restrained and locked in the chains that hung from the ceiling.

'Welcome to Cerasgrad, little lady,' chuckled one of the guards as he began to whip Raevyria while the other two began to beat her, laughing while doing so. The pain of her flesh being torn was excruciating. Raevyria tried to contain her pain, but the whippings and the beatings were too unbearable. Tears began to stream uncontrollably down her face as the guards continued to whip and beat her. To the guards' surprise, Raevyria's Heartcrux triggered her Crysterial Progression, which began to heal all her injuries and transformed the deep gashes from the whipping into thin crystal scars. Because of this, the guards spent hours torturing her, and her screams reverberated throughout the entire fortress.

The guards laughed when their playtime of torture was done, and they promised to see Raevyria again soon before departing the cell and locking the door behind them. Raevyria's white dress was drenched in blood, the pain of the whippings and the beatings throbbed throughout her entire body. Everything hurt. Seeing the bloodstains on her dress made Raevyria think about Denavayda and Belvafreya. She missed them. She wanted to see them, especially Denavayda. Raevyria wrapped herself in blankets and sobbed.

'Raevyria? Are you okay?' asked Zelderaph, concerned, but Raevyria did not respond and continued to sob.

A few moments of silence later, Raevyria heard one of the slabs on the cold floor begin to move. Surprised, Raevyria jumped back and pressed herself against the wall. The slab scraped across the floor and from a hole underneath it appeared a man in his mid-twenties. He was an exceedingly handsome man with long black hair that reached to his waist, pale skin, and beautiful amethyst eyes. He was attired in a white bloodstained shirt and wore baggy pants covered in dirt.

'Hello,' smiled Zelderaph softly, 'You didn't respond so I came to check on you.' Raevyria looked bewildered,

'But? How?' gasped Raevyria in shock,

'I've been working on a network of tunnels for quite a while now,' said Zelderaph as he sat himself beside Raevyria, 'But it turns out the outer wall of the fortress has some protective charm on it, so I've never been able to break through… I've met a few prisoners in the process though.' Zelderaph wrapped his arm around Raevyria's shoulders and pulled her towards him. Initially she resisted, but when she felt his warmth, it reminded her so much of Denavayda, and she missed him terribly. Raevyria allowed herself to collapse in Zelderaph's arms and she cried her eyes out, 'For someone so young you are incredibly brave,' whispered Zelderaph softly, 'You should be proud of yourself.'

'I've got nothing to be proud of,' cried Raevyria, 'I'm a Crysteor who couldn't even protect her friends let alone herself. They are both dead, I've been kidnapped, and now the end of my life has begun.'

'Not necessarily,' mused Zelderaph, 'If you're really a Crysteor you could form Covenants.' Raevyria looked up at Zelderaph, confused.

'What do you mean?' asked Raevyria curiously. Zelderaph patted Raevyria on the head and stood up.

'The former occupant of this cell had many interesting theories,' said Zelderaph as he pointed to the walls. Raevyria had only just noticed that the walls of her cell were etched with writings and drawings, 'One of which was the Crysteors and their Crysteri.'

'Crysteri? What is that?'

'That's the name he gave to people who form Covenants with Crysteors,' said Zelderaph, 'The idea is the Crysteor would give a Crysteri part of their power in exchange for their life-force... the occupant of this cell muttered that, a long time ago, a Crysteor was able to survive dying altogether by forming many Covenants and having several Crysteri at once, but they all disappeared.' Raevyria looked all around at the etchings on the walls, completely baffled by what she had just heard. In the Crystaverse she was told that Crysterial Progression was the end-of-life stage for a Crysteor and that nothing could have been done to prevent it. 'According to the guy who was here before you,' added Zelderaph, 'A Covenant must be forged from a powerful bond between the Crysteor and the Crysteri or else it won't work.'

'A bond?' Raevyria mused, 'If this is true, I wonder why the Crystaverse didn't tell us this.'

'Don't overthink it, Raevyria,' said Zelderaph reassuringly, 'Maybe they don't know about it, after all, these are just theories from a former prisoner.'

'What happened to the prisoner that was here before?' asked Raevyria,

'No idea,' shrugged Zelderaph, 'One day he was here and the next he was gone. According to the guards he went to serve the Supreme Corruptor and his family, but I don't tend to take what the guards say as gospel truth…however, they didn't lie about you, so maybe he did go to serve the Darkaenian Family.' Raevyria suddenly remembered the Jester that was with Xeropheers and the Darkaenian warrior.

'The Jester!' gasped Raevyria. Zelderaph looked at Raevyria confused,

'Jester?' Zelderaph asked curiously,

'When the Darkaenian Supremacy came to Sacregard, there was a Jester there with Xeropheers and his brother,' said Raevyria. The thought of Xeropheers and his brother made her blood boil,

'Prince Xeropheers was there?' asked Zelderaph,

'And his murderous brother,' hissed Raevyria angrily with clenched fists, 'I swear the next time I see him I will kill him for what he did.'

'What did he do?' asked Zelderaph curiously,

'He killed my best friends,' replied Raevyria, 'And then he killed me.'

'I'm sorry you went through that,' said Zelderaph softly.

'Thank you,' sighed Raevyria, 'All Corruptors deserve to die.'

'All of them?' asked Zelderaph, 'Including me?' Raevyria looked at Zelderaph aghast.

'You're a Corruptor?' said Raevyria, shocked.

'Yes, I'm a Corruptor,' said Zelderaph sullenly, 'Almost all beings born in Darkaeus are Corruptors.' A few awkward moments of silence passed between Raevyria and Zelderaph before the latter approached the hole in the ground and made his way through it, leaving Raevyria all alone in her cell.

Raevyria felt awful. She did not mean to offend Zelderaph, but she could not forgive the Corruptors that killed her friends and ruined her life. She was not sure whether she should follow Zelderaph through the hole and apologize or leave him be. As she contemplated what to do next, she observed the etchings and the drawings on the walls and discovered that one of the walls was covered in names.

RAYAZARU FAEYRORAH LEVIATHAS TEMPEREST DARKAEON
DHINZERVEL WRAITHEN DREAMEUS NIGHTHIER GLORYPHEUS
ZELDERAPH EMERIS MILLOW ARTHORIANA CHANEDRAVELDA
LOKARAVENTU KEIRAVERE TERAPHAI SERCES PANDAEMON
UMBRIETTE GORDENLIA WINTORYA BENRA'DHIN YSABETH
JOELSEPH ZELODY ORCAS QEANA XYDANE RAEVYRIA
DENAVAYDA BELVAFREYA ASHAVERIDA

Most of the names Raevyria did not recognize, but some she did. She noted Demethari's name written on the wall, as well as Denavayda, Belvafreya and Zelderaph's names. As she looked through the names, she found her own etched into the wall with an arrow pointing downward beneath it. Raevyria followed the arrow to one of the dirty slabs on the floor against the wall and noticed that the slab was uneven and had been moved. She lifted the slab up and discovered a tattered letter attached to a worn and torn book. Raevyria was shocked to read that the letter in the book was addressed to her.

To dearest Raevyria aka Little Reverie

You're going to be here for some time, three years at most. Here's a bit of

reading for you to pass the time, you might find it intriguing or horrifying.

Keep Zelderaph close, you are going to need him, and he is going to need you.

The Jester

Master of Prophecies

'Little Reverie', that was a nickname Raevyria had not been called in a very

long time. The matrons and the children at the orphanage Raevyria once lived

with used to call her 'Little Reverie' for her childhood tenderness to daydream.

Raevyria scanned through the book and discovered it was full of notes and

drawings.

As Raevyria was looking through the book, she heard Zelderaph's door

unlock, and the guards enter his cell.

'Come on Zelderaph, time for your daily 'constitutional',' chuckled the guard

as the other two guards restrained him and dragged him out of his cell.

'Constitutional?' Raevyria wondered. What did the guards mean by that?

Raevyria did not know what was going on but while she was waiting for the

guards to return Zelderaph to his cell, Raevyria fell asleep, holding the book left

for her by the Jester. Several hours later, Raevyria was awoken by the sound of

the guards returning Zelderaph to his cell and locking the door behind them as the sound of their laughter trailed off into the distance. Raevyria approached the wall adjacent to Zelderaph's cell and spoke.

'Zelderaph? Are you alright?' Raevyria asked, concerned. Zelderaph did not respond. Worried, Raevyria climbed through the hole in the floor, crawled through a narrow tunnel, removed the uneven slab above her and appeared in Zelderaph's cell. When she appeared in his cell, she noticed massive claw marks scratched into the walls and blood stains everywhere. As she observed her new surroundings, she noticed that, curled up in the far corner of the room, was a large black furry creature whimpering and growling. 'Zelderaph? Is that you?' asked Raevyria worriedly as she cautiously approached the black, furry creature. The creature raised its head and looked at Raevyria and she discovered that the creature was a large wolf who possessed the same beautiful amethyst eyes as Zelderaph.

'Go away,' said the wolf, it possessed Zelderaph's voice.

'Zelderaph, please don't push me away,' said Raevyria softly, 'Are you alright? Did the guards do this to you?'

'Did the guards do *what* to me exactly?' asked Zelderaph angrily as he raised himself up onto his paws, his wolf form was almost the same height as Raevyria, 'Turn me into a wolf? Don't be ridiculous, I'm a Twi'lycan.'

'I'm sorry a what?' asked Raevyria baffled.

'A Twi'lycan,' repeated Zelderaph frustratedly, 'A creature with the ability to see and communicate with spirits, also in this form I can pass into the Interdimensional Realm of Spiritus.'

'That's incredible,' said Raevyria, genuinely impressed,

'My mother was a Twi'lycan,' said Zelderaph sullenly, 'Twi'lycanthropy was her last gift to me, the first being my life...she died giving birth to me.'

'I'm so sorry,' said Raevyria softly, 'So you are a Corruptor and a Twi'lycan?'

'Yes,' replied Zelderaph, 'Does that make you want to kill me even more? Do you wish me to die?' Raevyria felt immense guilt for having said what she did about all Corruptors deserving to die. Zelderaph had been nothing but kind to her.

'No, of course not,' said Raevyria as she sat beside Zelderaph's wolf form and stroked his head, 'Can you change back?'

'Yes, I can,' said Zelderaph, 'I can change whenever I want, it just takes a lot of energy.'

'Where did the guards take you?' asked Raevyria curiously.

'Where? I have no idea,' said Zelderaph shamefully, 'It happens every day, I get taken somewhere and I return to my cell as either a human or a Twi'lycan...I don't know what they do to me, but I always feel tired and exhausted afterwards.' Zelderaph then curled himself into a ball and closed his eyes, 'I'm sorry, but I need to rest.'

'Okay, I will leave you to sleep,' whispered Raevyria as she sat up and made her way towards the tunnel.

Chapter Six

The Master of Prophecies

Raevyria spent her first night in Cerasgrad sat in the corner of her cell, wrapped in blankets as she began to read the book left to her by the Jester, the self-proclaimed 'Master of Prophecies'. The book was very insightful, as well as being quite educational, as it began with a story.

Once upon a time, Ultraeos was full of worlds, each one unique and beautiful beyond imagination. The worlds of Ultraeos lived in peace and harmony for thousands of years, until the Beast of the Beyond appeared.

The Beast of the Beyond was the greatest threat Ultraeos had ever known. No one knew its real name, but it was believed that this creature, this 'Sovereign of Monstrosities' as it would become known as, emerged from the primordial shadows of the universe with its ethereal plague known as 'Sinscourge' and corrupted anyone and anything that got in its way. Sinscourge transformed all those who touched it into mindless and horrendous monsters, all bent to the Beast of the Beyond's will. These amassed creatures became known as 'Sinscourged' and served as the Sovereign of Monstrosities' personal army.

With this army of Sinscourged by its side, the Beast invaded Ultimate Destiny. Ultimate Destiny was a sentient dimension and the source of all power and knowledge, The Promised Paradise and the High Creator. Having successfully

invaded Ultimate Destiny, the Beast of the Beyond became the new ruler of a

tainted and corrupted cosmos, bringing about an age of fear and terror that

became known as 'the Scourge'.

Without Ultimate Destiny, the peoples of the worlds were powerless against the

Beast of the Beyond and its legions of Sinscourged.

In response to this threat, the Onceway, a mysterious and ubiquitous power,

instinctively bore an order of preternatural warriors that could combat the

Beast's mass of monsters and abominations; the Crysteors.

The Crysteors fought valiantly against the Beast of the Beyond's hordes, but

they did not have the power to destroy the Beast itself. Hoping to stop the Beast

of the Beyond once and for all, Glorypheus, the mightiest of all the Crysteors,

sacrificed himself to create a prison for the Beast of the Beyond in the schism

between time and space, and trapped it in there, liberating Ultimate Destiny

from its control. Free from the tyranny of the Beast of the Beyond and inspired

by the actions of the heroic Crysteor, Ultimate Destiny gathered the remaining

worlds of the fallen Ultraeos and converged them into three worlds; Old

Wonderearth became the seat of power for a new order of Immortal Gods that

became known as the Stories Once Told, the new deities of the Onceway. The

second world, Foreverearth, became the home for the surviving peoples of

Ultraeos. To aid the Crysters in defending Foreverearth, Ultimate estiny created the Eldalongs, the first dragons, to help the Crysteors protect the realms of Foreverearth and warden over the Gate of Neverearth, the third world that would serve as the Beast\of the Beyond's eternal prison.

Ultimate Destiny also created Wraithen, the Lady of Life and Death, who watched over the Living and the Dead with the mysterious Twi'lycans, who served as Wraithen's emissaries in Ultimate Destiny's absence, and wardens of the interdimensional Realm of Spiritus.

Content with the creation of the new worlds, the imprisonment of the Beast of the Beyond and knowing that the worlds and the Onceway were in the safe hands of the Crysteors, the Eldalongs, Wraithen and the divine Stories Once Told, Ultimate Destiny disappeared, never to be seen again.

For a while peace and prosperity reigned in the world of Foreverearth, under the protection of the Crysteors and the Eldalongs. The Crysteors took the Central Realm of Sacregard as their own to serve as their home and stronghold, while the Eldalongs each took residence in Six of the Nine Realms of Foreverearth, becoming Sovereign Deities.

Rayazaru, the Lord of Light and Harmony, took the Northern Realm of Luxdanion and lived among the humans. He established a religion known as the Sanctuary and taught his followers, the Confessors, to embrace their inner Holylight and use it to spread peace across the world.

Faeyrorah, the Earthmother and Grandmother Time, became the guardian of the Northeastern Realm of Elvarorah and the Elfaery people. The Elfaery created a protective order known as the Li'ay to guard Faeyrorah, the World Forest, and protect the peoples of Elvarorah.

Leviathas, the Mistress of the Water and Memories, rose to rule the Eastern Realm of Aqualasia and lived there with the Aquara.

Darkaeon, the Prince of Darkness and Chaos, resided in the Southern Realm of Darkaeus and secluded Himself from the rest of the world.

Temperest, the Judge of Storms and War, lived in the Southwestern Realm of Ghalatel among the nomadic desert Darshans Chiefs and Djinns.

And Dhinzervel, the King of Fire and Desire, took the Western Realm of Valarvaal for his own and existed there with the Furyvires. The Cerulean Furyvires established the Emberwill Empire to protect Dhinzervel and rule His people while the Crimson Furyvires served as soldiers and warriors for the Crysteors.

With the Eldalongs serving as Sovereign Deities of their respective Realms and the Crysteors as the protectors of Foreverearth, the world existed in an era of peace and tranquility for nearly a thousand years. Everything seemed blissful, that is, until a dark shadow from the south began to slowly spread.

From the Southern Realm of Darkaeus rose the Corruptors, those with the abnormal power to control and spread Sinscourge, who made it their purpose to find the Beast and return it to their former glory as ruler of all Ultraeos. The Corruptors slaughtered the Eldalong of Darkaeus, Darkaeon, and established an autocratic authority known as the Darkaenian Supremacy, under the rule of the one they called the Supreme Corruptor, and with their influence over the Sinscourge they became the new masters of the Beast's legion of Sinscourged. With these monsters under their control, they began their search for the legendary Beast.

For millennia the Crysteors fought against the rising forces of the Darkaenian Supremacy, all the while protecting and guarding the Beast's prison, until one devastating day the seal on the Beast's prison broke, and the Sovereign of Monstrosities was once again free roam the world. Prioritizing revenge above all else, the Beast sought to destroy the Crysteors and the world that had imprisoned it for so long. Aligning itself with the autocracy that worshipped it so much, the Beast waged war across all the Realms of Foreverearth and sought to destroy everyone and everything.

Faithful to their Pledge, the Crysteors revolted against the Beast and the Darkaenian Supremacy. The mighty warriors vowed not to let the sinister Beast's obsession become a universal ambition. The Crysteors made great personal sacrifices to reseal the Beast within its prison beyond the Gate of

Neverearth and beat the legions of the Darkaenian Supremacy back to the Realm of Darkaeus. Knowing that the Darkaenian Supremacy would not stop, the Crysteors decided to hide the Gate of Neverearth and maintain it with a stronger seal. They made a solemn oath to the peoples of the world, and to themselves, that the Beast would not break free and cause so much pain and suffering again.

For thousands of years the Crysteors kept vigil over the Gate of Neverearth, its true location only known to a select few. As time passed, the seal of the Beast's prison once again began to weaken, not only that, but the Crysteors also began to dwindle as the Crysteors eventually realized that their power and their destinies came at a terrible price.

A terrible price? Could that be Crysterial Progression? Raevyria felt that she had learned more about the Crysteors and the World she lived in from the Jester's book than she did in the six years she lived at the Crystaverse. The Beast of the Beyond? The Gate of Neverearth? Raevyria had never heard of any of these things before. Raevyria remembered the nightmares she had about the monster that rose from the crumbling grounds of the Crystaverse. She also recalled Auraedeus Auramaedes mention the 'Gate Chamber' – could the Gate that the Prime Crysteor had been referring to be the Gate of Neverearth? Raevyria had so many questions and no one to answer them. She missed

Demethari, she missed Belvafreya, but most of all she missed Denavayda. She wanted to go home.

As Raevyria was fondly reminiscing about her time in Sacregard, she did not notice that Zelderaph had appeared in her cell and was back in his human form.

'Morning,' said Zelderaph softly, 'How are you feeling today?'

'I couldn't sleep,' said Raevyria as she wiped away the tears from her face,

'Yes, the first night is always the worst,' said Zelderaph reassuringly. That was exactly what Belvafreya said to Raevyria after her first night in Sacregard. Tears filled her eyes and began to stream down her face as she thought about her beloved friends. 'I'm sorry, I didn't mean to upset you.'

'You didn't,' said Raevyria, 'I'm just missing home and my friends.'

'Must be nice to have a home,' mused Zelderaph, 'All I've ever really known is this place.'

'You've never had a home?'

'Well, if I did, I don't remember it.'

'I'm sorry, Zelderaph,'

'Don't be, how can I miss something I've never had? Anyway, what's that?' Zelderaph then pointed to the book in Raevyria's lap.

'I found it underneath a loose slab by that wall of names over there,' said Raevyria, 'It was addressed to me and signed by 'The Jester, Master of Prophecies',' Raevyria handed Zelderaph the letter and the book.

''Master of Prophecies?'' said Zelderaph thoughtfully as he examined the letter and the book, 'Looks like he knew he was going to be a servant for the Darkaenian Family, and he knew you were going to be captured and placed in this cell. And he left this book specifically for you? I must admit, that is very impressive.'

'But why me?' asked Raevyria, 'What's special about me?'

'I can think of a few things,' smiled Zelderaph, 'But maybe this book will have the answers you seek. He must have left it to you for a reason. All I can suggest is to read it and find out.'

'I've already begun reading it,' said Raevyria as she took the book and the letter back from Zelderaph, 'And there's a story about a Beast in it.'

'The Beast of the Beyond?' asked Zelderaph curiously. Raevyria nodded, surprised Zelderaph knew that 'Every Corruptor in Darkaeus knows the story about the Beast of the Beyond and how it once took over all of Ultraeos by invading Ultimate Destiny before being stopped by Glorypheus. Apparently the Darkaenian Supremacy was built on the remains of the Beast of the Beyond's former home before it invaded Ultimate Destiny.'

'But what *is* Ultimate Destiny?' asked Raevyria.

'It's exactly what the book says,' shrugged Zelderaph, 'It is the High Creator of Ultraeos, the source of everything. The Sanctuary in Luxdanion revere Ultimate Destiny and refer to it as "The Promised Paradise" and believe it to be the place virtuous and good people go to once they die. Before my mother died, she told me that Wraithen guides the Holylight of people who have died to Ultimate Destiny from Spiritus so they can either be reborn or become one with Ultimate Destiny.'

'That's incredible…' gasped Raevyria, 'Can such a thing really exist?'

'Possibly,' said Zelderaph, intrigued, 'It wouldn't surprise me. But Ultimate Destiny's physical form disappeared so long ago there are those who even question its existence.' Raevyria sat and pondered for a moment,

'Do you believe it is real?' asked Raevyria.

'I do,' said Zelderaph, 'I believe it is out there somewhere, and I think that, even though it is no longer here we are call connected to Ultimate Destiny. I reckon the Stories Once Told know where it is.' The Stories Once Told? Raevyria remembered reading about them in the Jester's story, they were the divine entities that dwelt on the World of Old Wonderearth, 'Anyway, I'd keep that book safe if I were you, if the Jester wanted you to have it then there must be for a reason. Maybe it's written in there.'

Suddenly, the door to Raevyria's cell began to unlock. Swiftly, Zelderaph made his way to the hole and covered it with the slab while Raevyria hid the book and the letter in her ruffled blankets. The three guards from the previous day appeared, grinning, and laughing maniacally as they grabbed hold of Raevyria and locked her in the chains that dangled from the ceiling. The beatings and the whipping went on for hours, the guards seemed to enjoy torturing someone who could instantly heal her injuries, but the more times she healed herself, the more her Heartcrux began to pain her. Almost the entirety of Raevyria's back was covered in crystal scars by the time the guards had finished with her. They promised to see her tomorrow before unchaining Raevyria, leaving the cell and locking it behind them. Raevyria collapsed to the floor, holding her chest. As soon as the guards left, Zelderaph, who had been watching the entire ordeal, emerged from the hole, and held Raevyria tightly in his arms. Zelderaph's presence was a huge comfort to her, and, for the first time, she hugged him back and cried in his arms.

'According to the letter,' whispered Zelderaph as he held onto Raevyria, 'You only have to endure this for three years…I don't know what is going to happen, but until then, I'll be with you.'

'Do you promise?' sobbed Raevyria,

'I promise.' Zelderaph said as he tightened his embrace and pulled her closer.

Zelderaph was true to his word. Every day for the next three years he would visit Raevyria in her cell and comfort her after her daily torment. And when he returned from his regular 'constitutionals', Raevyria would visit Zelderaph in his cell and offer comfort when he was in either his human or Twi'lycan forms.

When Raevyria was not with Zelderaph she would continue to read the book left to her by the Jester, the Master of Prophecies. As she read the book, she continued to learn more about the Crysteors. According to the Jester's book, all Crysteors were conceived by the Onceway and only had birth mothers that died during childbirth. That explained why Raevyria never knew her birth parents. She also learned that all Crysteors were infertile, and that no child had ever been born to a Crysteor before. The knowledge that she would never be a mother hurt and upset Raevyria.

Not only did Raevyria learn more about the Crysteors, but she also learned more about the Darkaenian Supremacy. According to the Jester's book, the Darkaenian Supremacy had an uneasy alliance with the Emberwill Empire of the Western Realm of Valarvaal and that they had Cerulean Furyvires at their disposal. The Darkaenian Supremacy also possessed experimental technology, such as the Confinement Armour that imprisons its victim in a suit of armour that takes away all sense of self and makes them bound to the Darkaenian Family's will.

The final pages of the book contained various prophecies, some that did not make sense to Raevyria. However, there was one prophecy that stood out to Raevyria the most, as it was addressed to her.

Raevyria, Little Reverie, in your third-year fire will rain and love will be lost and regained.

Fire will rain and love will be lost and regained? Raevyria did not understand what the prophecy meant but she assumed that the third year referred to her third year of being in Cerasgrad.

On her eighteenth birthday, the guards came to inflict their daily torment on Raevyria, but just as they were about to strike her, Zelderaph emerged from the hole and beat the guards the unsuspecting guards to death with his bare hands. He grabbed the keys from one of the guards and freed a horrified Raevyria from her chains.

'Zelderaph!? What did you--?' exclaimed Raevyria, but before she could finish her sentence Zelderaph had softly planted a kiss on her lips.

'I'm not going to let anyone hurt you ever again,' whispered Zelderaph as he continued to kiss Raevyria, 'I'll kill every guard that comes through that door.' Zelderaph's kisses, his touch, his warmth, his words, everything about him made Raevyria's heart and stomach flutter as she melted into his arms and reciprocated the passionate kisses. They pulled their bodies closer to each other and, the next thing they knew, they were both undressing each other and lying naked on the blankets, making hard and passionate love to one another. When the love was made, they both fell asleep in each other's arms.

Raevyria had a beautiful dream of being in an endless field of beautiful Look-At-Me-Nots, a flower that shined in seven different colours, and found herself surrounded by floating orbs of iridescent Onceway. Raevyria looked around at the wisps of Onceway floating around and the flowers, entranced by their beauty. As she observed her surroundings, she came across a tall, hooded figure dressed in ghostly, iridescent robes holding two orbs of Onceway. One of the orbs of Onceway possessed a black aura while the other had golden light surrounding it. The black aura orb of Onceway floated out of the hooded figure's crystal hand and entered Raevyria's body closely followed by the Onceway that illuminated golden light. The feeling of the orbs entering her body felt warm, tingly, and reassuring. The hooded figure nodded before disappearing into iridescent stardust, leaving Raevyria alone in the field of Look-At-Me-Nots and the wisps of Onceway.

The peaceful sleep between the lovers did not last long, however, when large fireballs rained from the stormy skies and struck the fare side of Cerasgrad, causing a massive explosion that reverberated throughout the entire fortress. Raevyria and Zelderaph shot up, quickly put their clothes back on and looked outside through the small, barred window. The skies were red with crimson fireballs as they continued to strike and destroy Cerasgrad. Zelderaph saw one such fireball head straight towards them. Instinctively, Zelderaph grabbed hold of Raevyria and held her in a tight embrace and pinned her against the door as the fireball destroyed the wall. From the massive, fiery hole in the wall Raevyria could barely see the Furyvires of the Crimson Guard flying and launching fireballs at the crumbling prison. A figure landed in Raevyria's cell and through the smoke Raevyria saw a face that she had only dreamt about for the last three years.

It was Denavayda.

Raevyria's hearts soared when she saw the face of her beloved Denavayda. Without thinking, Raevyria leapt towards Denavayda and held him tightly, tears streaming down her face. She had never felt so happy. But Denavayda did not return the embrace as he began to sniff her. Without saying a word, Denavayda pushed Raevyria to the side and, armed with Tongue, he marched towards Zelderaph and pressed his sword against his neck.

'No! No! Denavayda stop!' pleaded Raevyria as she forced herself between Zelderaph and Denavayda, 'Please! He's a friend!'

'A *friend*, huh?' hissed Denavayda, 'Doesn't smell like it.'

'I suppose no one has ever told you that sniffing people is not only rude but gross too?' said Zelderaph indifferently. Denavayda pressed Tongue deeper into Zelderaph's neck, causing him to slightly bleed black ooze.

'A Corruptor?' growled Denavayda,

'Denavayda, please,' begged Raevyria, 'Please don't hurt him, without him, I'd have gone mad, I—'

'Do you have *any* idea how long I have been looking for you!?' said Denavayda angrily to Raevyria, 'From the moment I woke up from my coma I have been looking for you! I have searched all the Realms of Foreverearth looking for you! This place, *this place*, is literally the last place I have looked! As soon as I found out about this prison, I came for you! And what do I find!? You are here with a Corruptor!' In his anger, Denavayda's eyes began to glow, and he punched a fireball into the wall adjacent to Zelderaph's cell. Raevyria's heart sank. Denavayda had been in a coma and had spent the last three years doing nothing but search for her? A wave of guilt spread throughout the entirety of Raevyria's body.

'I'm sorry…' cried Raevyria, 'I'm so sorry.'

'What are you sorry for?' asked Zelderaph, 'You've got nothing to be sorry for.' A few awkward moments of silence passed between the three. Denavayda lowered Tongue and sheathed it. Zelderaph approached Raevyria and pulled her into an embrace. 'Thank you Raevyria, thank you for making these last three years bearable. But I think you should go with your friend, go home, and regain your lost time.'

'No! I'm not going without you! You're coming with us!' insisted Raevyria. Zelderaph planted a kiss on Raevyria's forehead and stroked her face then placed Jester's book in her hands.

'Don't worry about me, we shall see each other again,' said Zelderaph reassuringly.

'Do you promise?'

'I promise.'

As Raevyria and Zelderaph were saying their goodbyes, the doors burst open, and several guards appeared armed with swords. Zelderaph transformed into his wolf form and began attacking the guards as Denavayda stepped forward to protect Raeveyria.

'Go!' shouted Zelderaph as he began mauling the guards. Not waiting a second more, Denavayda scooped Raevyria in his arms and flew off towards a Sacregardian airship.

When Raevyria and Denavayda landed on the deck of the ship, Denavayda instantly put her down, walked past a welcoming Demethari and marched off to the cabins, slamming the doors behind him. Demethari, though baffled by Denavayda's behaviour, raced to Raevyria and welcomed her with a warm embrace.

'My dear Raevyria,' said Demethari softly, 'My dear girl, are you alright?' Raevyria broke down into tears as Demethari tightened his embrace, 'It's alright,' the aged Elfaery said reassuringly, 'Let's take you home.'

Chapter Seven

The Gate Chamber

The news of Cerasgrad's destruction did not take long to reach the Darkaenian Palace. When the news reached the Supreme Corruptor, Mortipher, he was furious, but when Prince Xeropheers heard about it, he was unfazed and slightly amused. The Senate of Lord Corruptors sat uneasily as the Supreme Corruptor's anger escalated,

'How could this happen!?' raged the Supreme Corruptor as he killed a nearby guard with his sword. 'Was nobody on sentry duty!? Is Cerasgrad run by incompetent fools!? Someone explain to me how this could have happened!?'

'It appears as though Furyvire Fire was able to penetrate the Prison's defensive barrier,' said one of the Lord Corruptors,

'You *think*!?' bellowed Mortipher sarcastically,

'Father, would it reassure you if I told you this was meant to happen?' asked Xeropheers nonchalantly. Mortipher redirected his anger to his son,

'What!?' said Mortipher angrily,

'The attack on Cerasgrad was one of the Jester's prophecies,' said Xeropheers calmly as he pulled out a small book from his pocket and scanned through its pages, 'Ah here it is, right here. '*When fire rains it shall be said farewell to all at Cerasgrad*'.'

'And you're telling me this *now*!?' fumed Mortipher, 'Summon the Jester!' As ordered, the skeletal Jester staggered into the great hall of the Darkaenian Palace and stood before the Supreme Corruptor,

'Jester, your prophecies have aided and enlightened us for many years now,' said Xeropheers casually, 'Why did you not inform His Majesty of Cerasgrad's destruction?'

'I apologise,' said the Jester jovially, 'But I only reveal to His Majesty what is necessary, unless he wants to know everything like I know everything? Might drive His Majesty a bit potty if you get my lotty?' The Jester then laughed maniacally.

'Jester,' said Mortipher firmly, 'What do you know?'

'I just said, I know EVERYTHING!' laughed the Jester, 'I know everything about you! And you! And you! And you! You! You! You! You! I know everything and everything about everyone!'

'Tell us how we should proceed next,' ordered the Supreme Corruptor. The Jester stopped laughing and jumping around and pointed a spindly finger at the Supreme Corruptor.

'If you do not have a care, then command and summon Despair, there you will determine your fate, at the place where you will find the Gate,' smiled the Jester. Mortipher stared angrily at the Jester while Xeropheers looked curious,

'The Gate? The Gate of Neverearth? It's in Sacregard?' asked Xeropheers. The Jester did not respond, instead he opened the great hall doors and cartwheeled down the corridor, laughing maniacally.

'Supreme Corruptor? Are you seriously considering summoning Despair?' asked one of the Lord Corruptors cautiously, 'Summoning that creature takes a lot of energy and—'

'As the Supreme Corruptor I am the only one who can summon and control Despair,' said Mortipher firmly, 'I will summon it at once.'

When Raevyria saw the lights of Sacregard on the edge of the horizon, her heart soared. She was finally going home, but she could not help but worry about Zelderaph. She hoped that he was okay and that he had gotten out of Cerasgrad safely.

The airship landed in the Courtyard of the Crystaverse and for the first time in three years she was reunited with Scorch, who was more than happy to see her.

'Hello Scorch,' whispered Raevyria softly as she stroked her Starbird, 'I missed you too.' Demethari escorted Raevyria into the Crystaverse and ordered the servants to draw a bath for her. A bath. The thought of having a nice, warm bath exhilarated Raevyria, and once she got into the bath, it was a lot better than she had hoped. Raevyria spent a long time in the bath, washing the dry blood and dirt off her skin and caressing the crystal scars she received during her three-year imprisonment. She had been through a lot, but she would not have gotten through it if it was not for Zelderaph. She felt as though she owed him so much. Then she thought about Denavayda, and about what he said. He had been in a coma and had been searching for her for a long time. She loved Denavayda, but she loved Zelderaph too. Her heart was torn and broken for losing Zelderaph and causing Denavayda pain.

After enjoying her relaxing bath, Raevyria got changed into her nightgown and made her way to bed. Demethari put Raevyria up in her own bedroom as a new Crysteor had taken her old bed and she was now a Master, which came with special privileges including her own room. Although she was grateful for having her own space and her own room, she missed having company. She tried to sleep but she could not get herself comfortable. The bed was nice and soft, which was completely different to the cold hard floor she spent three years sleeping on. No matter how hard she tried, Raevyria could not sleep, so she wrapped a throw around herself, slipped her slippers on and went for a stroll in the Courtyard. She thought she was on her own, until they saw Denavayda tending to Scorch. Raevyria was unsure what to do, should she approach him or wait for him to come to her? Before she could decide Denavayda caught sight of her and made his way towards her.

'Denavayda, I-' Raevyria began, but Denavayda just brushed past her. 'Please Denavayda, talk to me,' said Raevyria as she followed Denavayda, 'I haven't seen you in so long, I missed you so much.'

'Obviously didn't miss me that much,' said Denavayda angrily as he came to a sudden stop and faced her,

'I thought you were dead!' cried Raevyria, 'I spent three years grieving for you and Belvafreya but…but… Zelderaph was there for me, he comforted me during the worst times and- '

'I lost my sister!' Denavayda shouted back, 'My *twin*! Do you have any idea what that is like!? And when I woke up, I was told I'd lost you too! The love of my…' Denavayda stopped himself, 'We can never have what we once had, not anymore. I will always love you…but I can only be your friend from now on.' Tears welled up in both Raevyria and Denavayda's eyes.

'I'm so sorry, Denavayda,' whispered Raevyria as she approached Denavayda and kissed his cheek. Just as she was about to return to her room, Raevyria heard an eerie voice calling her name.

'What's wrong?' asked Denavayda curiously as he noticed the perplexed look on Raevyria's face. 'What is it?'

'Did you hear someone call my name just now?' asked Raevyria,

'No, I didn't hear anything,' said Denavayda. The voice called Raevyria's name again. It sounded like it was coming from the ground, underneath the Crystaverse to be exact. Raevyria followed the sound of the eerie voice and Denavayda followed her. Raevyria followed the voice until it led her to a downward staircase with a crystal door at the end of it.

'What is this place? I've never noticed this before.' said Raevyria as she examined the crystal door. Before she could touch the door, another voice appeared from the top of the staircase.

'What are you two doing?' asked the voice curiously. Startled, Raevyria and Denavayda turned to discover Demethari at the top of the stairs observing them.

'Master Demethari, what is this place?' Raevyria asked. Sensing this was a Crysteor matter, Denavayda left the two alone and bid them both goodnight before returning to his room.

'This…' began Demethari as he descended the stairs towards Raevyria, 'This is the Gate Chamber.' Raevyria looked shocked,

'The Gate Chamber? This room contains the Gate of Neverearth?' Raevyria asked astonished. Demethari looked at Raevyria in surprise,

'How do you know about that?' said Demethari firmly while giving Raevyria a suspicious look.

Raevyria then began to tell Demethari the story of her time in Cerasgrad. She recounted the day she met Zelderaph, the discovery of Jester's book and what it contained, the daily torment she endured and Denavayda's rescuing her. She omitted her personal feelings for Zelderaph and Denavayda. Raevyria took Demethari to her room and showed him the book.

'This is the book?' mused Demethari. Raevyria nodded, 'How extraordinary. The gift of prophecy is a rare ability to have, even amongst the Crysteors, but for a Corruptor to possess such a gift, it's outstanding.'

'Master Demethari? Why did you not tell me about the Gate Chamber? About the Crysteri? The Eldalongs? Everything?' asked Raevyria,

'I was going to,' insisted Demethari, 'Once you were officially recognized as a Master, I was going to tell you everything as these are secrets shared only amongst the Masters. Who would have thought a prophetic Jester would have told you all this?'

'Can you tell me now? About the Gate Chamber?' said Raevyria.

'Of course, you deserve to know.' said Demethari, 'I will tell you everything. Let's return to the Gate Chamber first, then I will explain everything.'

As requested, Raevyria accompanied Demethari to the door of the Gate Chamber and, with a wave of his wands, the crystal that encased the door disappeared to reveal a large black door adorned with gold and silver locks. From his pocket Demethari removed a set of keys and began rummaging through them until he found the correct ones that unlocked the door. Demethari opened the door, took Raevyria by the hand, and they both entered the Gate Chamber. Raevyria found herself and Demethari at the top of a grassy, spiral slope and, several hundred feet down the centre of the spiral Raevyria saw a large, black gate oozing with Sinscourge and burning with flames that hissed and roared angrily.

'That is the Gate of Neverearth,' said Demethari, 'As you already know, many millennia ago, an ancient evil dominated the universe by invading Ultimate Destiny and tainting it with its power. A Crysteor, by the name of Glorypheus, single handedly managed to imprison the ancient evil, known as the Beast of the Beyond, in a schism between time and space that later became known as the Gate of Neverearth. Glorypheus perished but the Gate remains. Unfortunately, since Glorypheus' time, the seal has broken twice, and it required more sacrifices to maintain the seal. Last time the seal broke, we requested the help of the Eldalongs to strengthen the seal.'

'And did they? Help?' asked Raevyria curiously. Demethari nodded,

'They did,' said Demethari, 'But because it cost them a majority of their power, they refused to offer further assistance, so our current generation of Crysteor Masters have been contributing their power and their lifeforce into maintaining the seal.'

'I see,' said Raevyria thoughtfully, 'What about the Crysteri? Did you know about them?'

'I do,' said Demethari sullenly, 'The practice of creating Crysteri is now forbidden under the authority of the Prime Crysteor Auraedeus Auramaedes. You see, the creation of a Crysteri must be forged from a powerful bond, whether it is between friends, siblings, parents, lovers, it must be born from something powerful. Although the Crysteri can extend the life of a Crysteor, they are losing their own life in the process. Basically, the Crysteri will be dying in your place... would you want to lose someone you love like that?'

'No, I wouldn't,' said Raevyria,

'That is why it is no longer practiced and if you are caught creating Crysteri you will be in big trouble,' said Demethari firmly. Demethari then reached into his pockets and pulled out two familiar looking wands.

'My wands!' gasped Raevyria as she took them off Demethari's hands,

'Your wands maintained their continuous glow after your capture which was how we knew you were alive and needed to rescue you,' said Demethari,

'What do you mean my wands maintained their glow?' asked Raevyria.

'Did I not tell you? Your wands are made from your bones,' said Demethari nonchalantly, 'All Crysteors are born with a crystal skeleton which is what we use to craft the core of your wands.'

'When do you get to my bones!?' exclaimed Raevyria, horrified,

'On your first night here,' said Demethari. Raevyria was mortified, but looking back on it, she did remember feeling pain in her legs on her first night in Sacregard. So that was when they took the bones to make the core of her wands? Even though Raevyria was surprised, it all made sense. 'I'm sorry I didn't tell you any of this sooner. Believe me, I wanted to tell you, but you needed to be recognized as a Master for me to be able to indulge that information to you.'

'I understand,' said Raevyria, 'Thank you for telling me now... but Master, a while ago, I heard a voice calling my name.'

'I heard a voice calling my name too,' said Demethari, 'When you hear the voice of the Beast it usually means the seal in weakening, don't worry, I will sort it out now.' Unsheathing his wands, Demethari created a small crystal platform that levitated above the hole and stepped onto it. Kneeling, Demethari muttered a small incantation, pointed his wands at the Gate of Neverearth and unleashed a beam of Onceway at it, which settled down the hissing and the roaring that came from the Gate of Neverearth.

'What did you do?' asked Raevyria incredulously,

'I contributed my lifeforce to the seal,' said Demethari, 'That should keep the Beast at bay for now.'

'But why!? You're already experiencing Crysterial Progression, you should be taking better care of yourself!' exclaimed Raevyria. Demethari returned to Raevyria's side and patted her gently on the head.

'Thank you for your concern, Raevyria,' said Demethari softly, 'But I am more than content with contributing my life to this cause. If I am to die sealing the Beast away, then I will have done something useful with my life. That's more than enough for me.' Taking Raevyria's hand into his own, Demethari led the pair out of the Gate Chamber and sealed the door behind them.

As soon as Demethari resealed the Gate Chamber with crystal, the warning bells of the Crystaverse began to sound. Raevyria and Demethari raced up the stairs and made their way to the Courtyard, where they saw the flagship of the Darkaenian Supremacy's armada, *The Poisoned Duchess*, hovering above the perpetual barrier that protected Sacregard. Other Crysteors and members of the Crimson Guard gathered in the Courtyard and watched as the Supreme Corruptor himself, Mortipher Darkaenian, appeared on the deck and looked down at the Crysteors with his two sons, Prince Xeropheers and the Darkaenian warrior, stood beside him.

'Greetings Crysteors of Sacregard,' said Mortipher loudly, 'We are looking for a prisoner of ours and we believe she may be in your custody.' The Crysteors and the Crimson Guard began to chatter amongst themselves, 'If you hand the girl over now no one will be harmed, but if you fail to comply, I shall bring you Despair.' At the sound of its name, a large ghostly hooded figure shrouded in darkness and ethereal Sinscourge appeared from behind *The Poisoned Duchess*. The Crysteors armed themselves with their wands and prepared themselves for a fight, including Raevyria and Demethari. The large spectral being known as Despair floated above the barrier and, even though its eyes were concealed by the shadows of his hood, Raevyria could sense that the creature was observing the Crysteors, looking for her. Her suspicions were proven correct when Despair caught sight of Raevyria and pointed directly at her. Xeropheers stepped forward, observed the crowd of Crysteors and saw Raevyria.

'That's her,' said Xeropheers nonchalantly,

'Bring her to me,' said Mortipher firmly and at its Master's command, Despair reached its hand downward, phased through the barrier and reached towards Raevyria. As the hand penetrated the barrier, a flurry of light shot out from the wands of the Crysteors and beat the hand back behind the barrier.

Despair let out a horrific shriek, swooshed its entire being into the barrier and broke it into a million pieces, which allowed *The Poisoned Duchess* to land in the Courtyard. Despair shrieked again and charged towards the crowd of Crysteors. Many of the Crysteors were able to protect themselves by casting their own barriers around themselves while others were fatally knocked out by Despair's charge attack, causing their Heartcrux's to become exposed.

As the Crysteors attacked Despair and fought the horde of Sinscourged that suddenly appeared from *The Poisoned Duchess*, only Demethari noticed that whatever pain was inflicted on Despair also affected the Supreme Corruptor. He noticed the ruler of the Darkaenian Supremacy wince in pain at each blow that struck Despair. Raevyria assisted in the fight against Despair as she fired bolts of light from her wands at the large spectral being. As the Crysteors were attacking Despair and fighting the Sinscourged, both Xeropheers and the Darkaenian Warrior disembarked *The Poisoned Duchess* and engaged in individual duels with the Crimson Guard. The Crimson Guard fought valiantly against the Darkaenian brothers, but even their martial prowess and pyromancy was no match for the impressive swordsmanship of Xeropheers and the Darkaenian Warrior.

Denavayda arrived at the scene and initially wanted to help Raevyria and Demethari attack Despair, but anger and rage engulfed his being into flames at the sight of the Darkaenian Warrior, the one that killed Belvafreya and kidnapped Raevyria. Without hesitation Denavayda flew towards the Darkaenian Warrior, armed with both Tongue and Tooth, and engaged in a ferocious sword fight with the Darkaenian Warrior. Denavayda was holding his own, striking at the Darkaenian Warrior violently while using his impenetrable wings to shield himself from the Darkaenian Warriors fatal blows. Xeropheers had finished dispatching a member of the Crimson Guard when he caught sight of the intense battle between Denavayda and the Darkaenian Warrior. Xeropheers smiled as he cleaned the blood off his longsword and swung his blade at Denavayda. Denavayda managed to block the sword with Tooth and found himself in a duel with both Xeropheers and the Darkaenian Warrior. Fighting the Darkaenian Warrior with Tongue, Xeropheers with Tooth and shielding himself with his wings, Denavayda was holding his own extremely well until a brief lapse in concentration caused him to be struck by Xeropheers on his leg.

Hearing Denavayda groan in pain, Raevyria stopped attacking Despair and saw both the Darkaenian Warrior and Xeropheers fighting Denavayda. Raevyria pushed her way through the Crysteors attacking Despair and made her way towards Denavayda. With a swish of her wand, she fired a ball of Onceway at Xeropheers, knocking him off his feet and another at the Darkaenian Warrior which struck his head and caused his helmet to fly off. Raevyria transformed her wands into katana swords as she charged towards the Darkaenian Warrior but when she saw his face her heart stopped for a moment, and her legs went numb as she fell to the floor and found herself staring at a familiar face.

Chapter Eight

The Crown Prince of Darkaeus

It was Zelderaph.

'No…' gasped Raevyria horrified, 'No, that's impossible!' Tears filled Raevyria's eyes, and her heart sank. The man she had spent three years imprisoned with, the man that gave her hope when she had none and the man that gave her love when she needed it most was Belvafreya's murderer, as well as her own murderer. Denavayda was also surprised, but Zelderaph looked blank and emotionless. Xeropheers howled with laughter,

'Is it impossible? Really?' said Xeropheers incredulously, 'You stupid girl. Have a think about it, seriously, think! Is it impossible or did you not really care enough to notice?' Raevyria's hearts broke. The more she thought about it the more she realized it was not impossible after all. The daily 'constitutionals' when Zelderaph was taken out of his cell, was this what he was doing?

'Zelderaph…is this some kind of joke?' cried Raevyria, devastated, but Zelderaph did not say a word and remained expressionless.

'No joke.' Said Xeropheers, 'Allow me to officially introduce you to Crown Prince Zelderaph Crescence Darkaenian, Heir to the Darkaenian Supremacy and my older half-brother.' Raevyria stared at Zelderapah with tears streaming down her face, but he remained blank and emotionless.

'Zelderaph…talk to me, tell me this isn't true!' pleaded Raevyria as she leapt to her feet and wrapped her arms around Zelderaph's neck, holding him in a tight embrace he did not reciprocate. 'It isn't true, if you're the Crown Prince then why were you imprisoned?'

'He can't hear you,' said Xeropheers casually. Raevyria looked at Xeropheers perplexed, 'It's the armour, shall we say, it puts him in a kind of trance? He doesn't know what he's doing but he does as he is told by either myself or father.' Raevyria then remembered reading about the Confinement Armour in Jester's book, was the Jester trying to tell her the truth even then and she just did not realise it? It all made sense now, 'By the way, I can answer your question for you: Why was he imprisoned? For his own safety, it's as simple as that, also the Jester said he needed to be there.'

'What? Why?' asked Raevyria concerned,

'Because of you, stupid girl,' said Xeropheers impatiently, 'For the exact reason why *you* needed to be there.' Raevyria was even more confused. 'Did you even bother to read all the prophecies in the book?' Raevyria's mind was wracked with questions. The book? The Jester's book? How did Xeropheers know about the Jester's book? Did the Jester tell him? Why would he know that? Also, why did she and Zelderaph need to be together? She did not understand. Before she could respond, the Jester appeared out of nowhere and placed his hands over Xeropheers' mouth.

'Shush! Shush! Shush! Shush!' said Jester, panicking, 'She has not met Nighthier and Dreameus yet! And she needs to figure it out on her own! Now shush! Shush! Shush! Shush! Shush!' Raevyria was even more confused. Nighthier? Dreameus? Who were they? Although she did not know them, their names did sound familiar and she soon remembered where from – the wall of names in her cell at Cerasgrad, Nighthier and Dreameus were two of the names etched into the wall by the Jester.

The Jester turned his attention to Raevyria and frantically slapped her off Zelderaph,

'Deeper Love is a greater connection that True Love, don't you think?' asked the Jester jovially as he then turned his attention to Denavayda and smiled widely, revealing his sharp, jagged teeth, 'Your children will know a Deeper Love beyond imagination, it will even change the world.'

'Get lost, Clown!' snapped Denavayda as he swung Tooth at the Jester, who cartwheeled out of its way while laughing maniacally.

'Temper! Temper!' laughed the Jester, 'That could get you KILLED one day! By the way, where is that Elfaery Demethari?' Raevyria was so caught up with Denavayda, Zelderaph, Xeropheers and the Jester that she had forgotten about Demethari. Suddenly, Demethari appeared behind Zelderaph, aiming his wands at his throat. The Jester feigned shock at the sight of this.

'Demethari!' screamed Raevyria, 'What are you doing?!'

'Fulfilling my duty as a Crysteor,' said Demethari, who was surprisingly calm, 'This is what we do Raevyria, you cannot let personal feelings interfere with your destiny.' Mortipher, seeing his eldest son's life being threatened, disembarked *The Poisoned Duchess,* and made his way through the battle-ridden Courtyard towards his sons.

'Foolish Crysteor,' sighed the Supreme Corruptor, 'The Darkaenian Supremacy will succeed in retrieving the Gate of Neverearth, it has already been prophesized, it is just a question of when, and once we have the Gate of Neverearth, we can finally be reunited with the true ruler of Ultraeos.'

'The Beast of the Beyond will never rise again!' shouted Demethari angrily, 'So long as the Onceway flows through my veins, the seal on the Gate of Neverearth will be maintained.'

'I see… so it is *your* Holylight that keeps the Sovereign imprisoned?' mused the Supreme Corruptor, 'Very well, Despair, Corrupt him.' As the Supreme Corruptor's command, Despair appeared before Demethari, placed the tip of its skeletal finger on his head and infused him with Sinscourge.

'No!' Raevyria screamed as she tried to rush to her Master's side, only to be stopped by Denavayda. Demethari's eyes became consumed with Sinscourge and black veins protruded from his body. Despair removed its finger from the elderly Crysteor's head and Demethari stood completely still and expressionless. Injured and weakened by the attacks that were inflicted on Despair, Mortipher fell to the ground and dispelled the spectral being.

'Now then…' panted Mortipher as he rose to his feet, 'I command you to lead us to the Gate of Neverearth.' Obediently, Demethari, in a trance-like state, turned and swayed his way towards the Crystaverse with Mortipher closely following behind him, staggering. Raevyria transformed her wands back to their original form and aimed them at Demethari, but before she could do anything to help cure her Master of Sinscourge Xeropheers grabbed Raevyria from behind and pressed a knife to her throat, with Zelderaph doing the same to Denavayda.

'Let's go for a little walk, shall we?' whispered Xeropheers as he urged Raevyria to move and follow Demethari and Mortipher. The Courtyard was full of the bodies of Sinscourged and crystalized Crysteors who gave their lives fighting the horde of Sinscourged and Despair. There were some survivors who were injured and being tended to by the servants of the Crystaverse. The Prime Crysteor, Auraedeus Auramaedes, was so focused on healing the injured that he did not notice Demethari leading the Supreme Corruptor into the Crystaverse.

Raevyria hoped and prayed that Demethari would fight through the hold of the Sinscourge and not lead the Darkaenians to the Gate Chamber, but Raevyria's hopes were dashed when the possessed Demethari led them straight to it and opened the Chamber with his wands. The Chamber doors opened and

Demethari led Mortipher, Raevyria, Xeropheers, Denavayda and Zelderaph inside. Once inside, Demethari created a crystal platform large enough for the six to stand on and made its way down toward the Gate of Neverearth. The closer they got to the Gate of Neverearth, the more anxious Raevyria became. Once they reached the Gate of Neverearth, Mortipher forced Demethari to his knees and commanded Zelderaph to lift the Corruption on the elderly Elfaery, which caused them both to scream in agony,

'Master Demethari are you alright?' said Raevyria panic stricken as she rushed to his side.

'Raevyria? How did we get-?' asked a confused Demethari, until the Supreme Corruptor interrupted him.

'Open the Gate,' ordered Mortipher as Zelderaph pressed a blade against the Elfaery's neck, 'Open the Gate of I will order Zelderaph to cut off your head.'

'I imagine he'd survive that,' mused Xeropheers, 'From the looks of him he is already in Crysterial Progression, he is technically immortal until the Crysterial Progression kills him, Father.'

'How inconvenient...' snarled Mortipher, 'Very well then, let's see what he can live through!' With a snap of his fingers, Zelderaph swung his sword and beheaded Demethari.

'MASTER DEMETHARI!' screamed Raevyria as tears streamed down her face as she watched her Master's head roll across the Gate of Neverearth. To her surprise, and horror, the head spoke to her as it rolled,

'Don't cry, Raevyria, everything will be alright,' said Demethari reassuringly. Raevyria and Denavayda were stunned.

'Does that not hurt you, Demethari?' wondered Denavayda,

'It's bloody agony you fool!' snapped Demethari. Zelderaph retrieved the head and placed it back on the Elfaery's body, which was reattached by the Onceway. As his head was reattached the Demethari's body, more of his face began to crystallize. Raevyria's hearts sank, her Master was almost completely crystal.

'Let's see if her head will roll as far?' said Xeropheers thoughtfully and he unseathed his own sword and approached Raevyria. Denavayda stood himself between Xeropheers and Raevyria, wielding Tongue defiantly at the Prince of Darkaeus.

'Why don't we see how far *your* head will roll?' hissed Denavayda. Raevyria's hearts fluttered, even though she had hurt him so much Denavayda was still willing to protect her. However, Mortipher marched towards Raevyria and prepared to break her neck.

'Stop! Stop!' begged Demethari, 'Leave the girl alone… I'll do as you ask.'

'Master Demethari don't!' pleaded Raevyria as she struggled to free herself from Zelderaph's tight grip.

'Raevyria...' said Demethari softly, 'I have lived a long and fulfilling life, teaching young Crysteors our ways. I have had many excellent students over the years, but I don't think I have had one as remarkable as you. I love you my dear girl, as if you were my own grandchild, and I will do anything for you.' Without a moment's thought, Demethari unsheathed one of his wands, muttered and incantation, and began to unlock the seals and locks on the Gate of Neverearth.

As Demethari was unsealing and unlocking to Gate of Neverearth Mortipher, Xeropheers, Denavayda, Raevyria and Zelderaph began to step away from the Gate as it began to glow and roar violently. As Demethari unsealed the final lock, the Gate began to open as darkness and violet lights emerged from the Gate. Mortipher and Xeropheers watched in amazement as a large stream of Sinscourge emerged from the Gate and began to swirl around in different shapes and sizes. The magnificent display of Sinscourge began to shrink and minimize and soon took a form that no one, not either Mortipher or Xeropheers was expecting.

The Sinscourge transformed into a tiny rabbit that let out a less-terrifying squeak.

Raevyria, Denavayda, Mortipher and Xeropheers looked flabbergasted while Zelderaph remained expressionless and Demethari began to laugh, however,

Mortipher did not find the funny side to it at all and, in a fit of rage, he destroyed the tiny rabbit with his own Sinscourge. he then looked down into the Gate and saw that the schism between time and space that had confined the Beast of the Beyond for many millennia…was gone.

'Master Demethari? What's going on?' asked Raevyria, completely perplexed. Demethari laughed and looked scornfully at Mortipher,

'You are an idiot and a fool, Supreme Corruptor,' said Demethari as he rose to his feet and stood before Mortipher, 'There once was a Beast here, but not anymore, all that remains is a fragment of its essence which we used to take on a 'formidable' form for you should you ever get this far. You will never find the Beast.'

'JESTER!?' bellowed Mortipher furiously.

'MAJESTY!?' Jester screamed as he mysteriously appeared out of nowhere, again.

'What's going on!?' demanded the Supreme Corruptor, 'You said the Beast would be here!'

'Did I!?' grinned Jester, 'Are you sure? Think again Your Majesty, did I specifically say, 'The Beast is hidden underneath Sacregard'? Did I? No! What I believe I said was "*If you do not have a care, then command and summon Despair, there you will determine your fate, at the place where you will find the*

Gate." You assumed the Gate of Neverearth was here and you were right, but I didn't say ANYTHING about the Beast! In fact, you completely missed the part you should have probably thought about the most!'

'What part!?' raged Mortipher,

'THIS PART!' laughed Jester as he leapt out of the way, allowing Zelderaph to pull Raevyria out of Mortipher's grip, grabbing the Supreme Corruptor by the throat and threw him into the Gate of Neverearth. Upon entering the gate, Mortipher's Sinscourge left his body and entered Zelderaph, knocking him unconscious, while his physical being was ripped apart by the essence of the Beast. The Jester laughed maniacally, 'Guess he determined his FATE and the place where he found the GATE!' Raevyria, Denavayda and Demethari looked bewildered, while Xeropheers smiled.

'What a fool,' said Xeropheers nonchalantly,

'What happened?' asked Raevyria, completely confused.

'You know what happened!' said the Jester impatiently, 'I told you earlier! Why does nobody listen to ME!?' He did? Raevyria wondered. When did he do that? All Raevyria could remember Jester tell her was that Deeper Love was a greater connection than True Love. Wait, was that it? Was Zelderaph able to break through the influence of the Confinement Armour because of his love for her? Raevyria's hearts swelled with love for him as she rushed over to his side and held him in her arms,

'Zelderaph? Zelderaph? Are you alright?' whispered Raevyria softly as she stroked his face and gave him a gentle kiss on his forehead. Zelderaph stirred and opened his eyes at Raevyria's touch.

'Raevyria...' he whispered, 'Are you alright? Are you hurt?'

'I'm fine, we're all fine,' said Raevyria reassuringly.

Xeropheers, with a snap of his fingers, summoned a horde of Sinscourged that materialized out of nowhere. Instinctively, Zelderaph jumped to his feet and wrapped his arms around Raevyria to protect her when Denavayda stood in front of the couple, armed with Tongue and Tooth and ready for conflict. Demethari unsheathed his wands and prepared himself for battle.

'Now then,' said Xeropheers calmly, 'Where is the Beast? If you don't comply, I will unleash this horde upon you all.'

'I don't know,' said Raevyria, 'I was made to believe it was here.'

'I'm sorry I tricked you Raevyria,' said Demethari apologetically before turning to Raevyria, 'The truth is the only Crysteor who knows where the Beast is hidden is –'

'They're not real,' said Zelderaph suddenly, 'The Sinscourged, they're all an illusion...' Raevyria looked at Zelderaph surprised. Denavayda put Zelderaph's

116

theory to the test, approached a Sinscourged and slice straight through it, it was indeed an illusion. Denavayda looked at Zelderaph, impressed.

'Good call,' said Denavayda, 'But why conjure illusions and not the real thing? Does the little Prince of Darkaeus not have any real power over them!?' Before any of them knew it, Xeropheers teleported behind Zelderaph and, with a swift swing of his sword, he beheaded Zelderaph.

'NO!' screamed Raevyria, her blood curdling cry obliterating the illusions around them. As Zelderaph's head rolled off his shoulders he whispered, 'I love you, Raevyria,' and a shroud of darkness and Sinscourge left his body and consumed Raevyria, knocking her unconscious.

Chapter Nine

Nighthier and Dreameus

'Hello? Hello? Hey, can you hear me?'

A voice Raevyria had never heard before echoed through the darkness as she came to. When Raevyria woke up, she found herself back in the endless field of Look-At-Me-Nots. She soon realized she was not alone, as watching over her was a boy around fifteen years of age with disheveled black hair, pale skin and dressed in black. A unique feature that the boy had was his heterochromia as his right eye was amethyst purple and his left eye was emerald green.

'Who are you?' asked Raevyria, 'Where are we?'

'Dream, she's awake,' said the boy indifferently as he stood up to his feet and walked away. His voice was familiar to the voice she had heard, but it was slightly deeper and raspier than the voice she heard.

'Then talk to her!' came another voice. That was it, that was the voice she heard before. This voice was jovial and sounded gentler. Another boy that had been identified as 'Dream' then appeared and bent down beside Raevyria. He looked almost identical to the boy that had just walked away, except he had blonde hair, his right eye was emerald green and his left amethyst purple, and he wore white instead of black, 'Hi, are you alright?'

'Where am I? Who are you?' asked Raevyria as she examined her surroundings.

'Oh right, sorry, I'm Dreameus and this is my brother Nighthier,' said the blonde-haired boy as he stood up and playfully grabbed his brother in a headlock.

'Get off me you idiot!' snapped Nighthier as he pushed Dreameus off him so hard that Dreameus went tumbling in the Look-At-Me-Nots. Raevyria looked surprised when she heard those names, the same names that were carved into her cell wall at Cerasgrad and who the Jester referred to before.

'You two are Nighthier and Dreameus?' Raevyria asked curiously. The two boys nodded, 'I was told I'd meet you both.'

'Really? How interesting,' mused Nighthier.

'Well meeting us was going to be inevitable,' said Dreameus, 'Whether it is here or in your world you were going to meet us eventually.'

'What do you mean?' said Raevyria.

'You'll see,' smiled Dreameus. Raevyria could not help but smile back, even though she had no idea who these two boys were, she felt very comfortable being with them.

'Where is this place?' asked Raevyria as she examined her surroundings, 'I've been here before, but I have no idea where this is.'

'Ask him,' said Nighthier as he gestured to his twin brother. Dreameus plucked a Look-At-Me-Not and handed it to Raevyria.

'That bit's kind of hard to explain,' said Dreameus, 'We're in a dream but it's also a real place, if that makes any sense?' Raevyria awkwardly smiled as she shook her head and took the Look-At-Me-Not from the boy. Dreameus laughed nervously, 'This is a real place, but it's happening in a dream. Whenever a person dreams, their consciousness is taken to a place that brings their dreams to fruition. That's what this place is.' Raevyria thought about Dreameus' explanation and what he was describing sounded a lot like one of the theories about Ultimate Destiny she and Zelderaph talked about three years ago, Zelderaph believed that every living thing was connected to Ultimate Destiny, and he believed that the connection existed in dreams, and that Ultimate Destiny was the place where everyone goes to when they dream.

'I see,' muttered Raevyria to herself, 'That sounds a bit like Ultimate Destiny.'

'Ultimate Destiny? So that's the name of this place,' mused Dreameus,

'Why didn't you know that idiot?' asked Nighthier coldly,

'I'm sorry I'm not good at explaining, we've not been born yet so I can't know everything straight away.' Said Dreameus nervously. Not been born yet?

What did that mean? Dreameus changed the subject, 'Anyway, it's nice to meet you properly, Raevyria.'

'How do you know my name?' asked Raevyria surprised.

'There's a lot of things that we know now, but I think once we're born, we'll probably forget,' said Dreameus softly, 'By the way, that flower I gave you? If you are ever in a dire situation and need any help, just hold that flower, call our names and we'll come and help you, but we can only do this once, okay?'

'One flower, one chance,' added Nighthier, 'Don't waste it.' At that moment the field of flowers began to fade and Dreameus and Nighthier began to disappear.

'What's happening?' asked Raevyria concerned as she reached out for Dreameus and Nighthier.

'Don't worry, said Dreameus reassuringly, taking one of her hands into his own, 'You're just waking up, that's all.'

'Remember, keep that flower safe, you might need us,' said Nighthier calmly, taking Raevyria's other hand into his as he and his brother disappeared into the darkness.

When Raevyria came to, she found herself in a dark, damp cell bound and chained to Demethari and Denavayda.

'Raevyria? Raevyria? Are you alright?' asked Demethari concerned. Raevyria groaned and nodded her head, 'Thank goodness.' Demethari sighed with relief,

'Where are we?' said Raevyria as she examined her surroundings, 'Where is Zelderaph?' An awful silence passed between the three captives as Raevyria patiently waited for an answer while Denavayda and Demethari exchanged an uncomfortable glance at one another.

'We're aboard *The Poisoned Duchess*,' said Demethari, 'As for Zelderaph, well, he's-,'

'I hope he is alright,' interrupted Raevyria worriedly, 'He has to be okay, he has to be,'

'He's dead Raevyria,' said Denavayda quickly, 'He's dead, okay? After his head was chopped off Xeropheers kicked his body into the Gate,'

'Denavayda please,' said Demethari softly, 'Be a bit more delicate and understanding,'

'I'm not going to sugar-coat the facts, he's dead and that's that, don't expect me to grieve for the Corruptor scum that killed my sister and took Raevyria from me,' As Denavayda was speaking, Raevyria began to silently weep and reflect on her time with Zelderaph. His smile, his intelligence, his comfort, his voice, his love, everything about him made Raevyria feel nothing but adoration for him, but now he was gone forever, and that broke her heart.

'I'm so sorry my dear girl,' said Demethari, 'I know he must have meant a lot to you, Denavayda told me about the two of you and, all I can say, is I am truly sorry for your loss,'

'I can't believe he's gone,' wept Raevyria. Then, out of the darkness of the holding cell, the Jester emerged, smiling. 'You! Did you know that this would happen!?' Raevyria asked angrily as she tried to charge towards the Jester, only to be held back by the chains that bound her to Demethari and Denavayda.

'Of course, I did,' smiled the Jester, 'I know everything about everything and everyone, there are no surprises for me!'

'You could've changed it!' shouted Raevyria angrily, 'You could've stopped it from happening!? Why didn't you!?'

'I cannot interfere with the way things have got to be,' chuckled the Jester,

'What does that even mean!?' demanded Raevyria, the Jester's jovial behaviour began to anger her more and more, so much so that she used the Onceway wandless to attack him from a distance, but not matter how many times she tried to attack him, the Jester leapt and cartwheeled out of the way.

'Raevyria stop!' said Demethari desperately, 'If you keep using the Onceway wandless you'll—'

"I DON'T CARE! I DON'T CARE! I DON'T CARE!' cried Raevyria as she continued to shoot balls of Onceway at the Jester, 'Zelderaph is gone! He's gone and I should've been able to save him I should've--'

'There was nothing you could have done,' said Denavayda calmly. The sound of Denavayda's voice snapped Raevyria out of her frenzy, 'I'm sorry you lost someone you loved, but life must go on. If you respect Zelderaph then you'll continue to live your life not only for yourself, but for him as well. And what about me? Do you think I want you to see you kill yourself for him? What about what I want?' Raevyria turned to Denavayda, her eyes flooding with tears that streamed down her face, 'You're not alone, I'm here for you, for as long as you need me, okay?'

'Denavayda...' said Raevyria warily, tired from crying, 'I'm sorry,'

'What does Xeropheers intend to do with us?' asked Demethari curiously to the Jester.

'I believe he intends to bring you to Darkaeus to face the consequences of your crimes," said the Jester nonchalantly,

'Crimes? What crimes?' asked Raevyria angrily,

'For murdering the Supreme Corruptor and his Heir!' laughed the Jester,

'What!?' exclaimed Raevyria, Denavayda and Demethari shocked,

'Xeropheers intends to torture and execute you before the Senate of Lord Corruptors and declare himself the new Supreme Corruptor,' said the Jester, 'Quite a clever one, that Xeropheers!'

'I take it you foresaw his treachery?' said Raevyria coldly,

'Of course!' said the Jester jovially, 'Everything is going the way it is supposed to be!'

'What are we supposed to do next?' asked Denavayda desperately, 'We can't be tortured and executed for something we didn't do!'

'Do not fret, as long as the five of you stick together, you will be fine!' laughed Jester as he disappeared into the shadows of the holding cell.

Raevyria, Denavayda and Demethari looked baffled. The five of them? What did that mean?

'The idiot can't count,' said Denavayda, 'There's three of us.'

'What did he mean "the five of us"?' wondered Demethari. Raevyria thought for a moment until she felt something small and warm in her hand. It was the Look-At-Me-Not Dreameus had given her in her dream. How was that possible? How could she have the flower with her? It was all a dream, or was it? Raevyria held the flower tightly in her hand and did not mention it to either Denavayda or Demethari.

The Poisoned Duchess arrived at the Darkaenian Palace where Xeropheers was greeted by the Senate of Lord Corruptors.

'Welcome back, Prince Xeropheers,' said the Lord Corruptors as they bowed their heads in respect.

'My father, Mortipher Darkaenian, and my brother, Zelderaph, have been murdered,' announced Xeropheers nonchalantly. The Senate of Lord Corruptors began to chat amongst themselves, panicked over the news that the Supreme Corruptor and his Heir are dead, 'I have the culprits aboard *The Poisoned Duchess*, as the new Supreme Corruptor I command that they are tortured and executed immediately.' The Senate of Lord Corruptors hesitantly nodded their heads in agreement and bowed to their new Supreme Corruptor, 'The culprits also have information on the location of the Sovereign of Monstrosities, make sure you get that information out of them before executing them.'

'It will be done, Your Majesty,' said one of the Lord Corruptors. Smiling, Xeropheers strutted past the Lord Corruptors and entered the Darkaenian Palace.

As Xeropheers entered the great hall, he saw the Jester sat on the throne of the Supreme Corruptor,

'Hello, "*Your Majesty*",' said the Jester mockingly, 'So this was your plan all along? To dispose of your father and brother and take the throne for yourself! Cheeky cheeky!'

'Not just my father and brother,' said Xeropheers casually, 'I also intend to kill that stupid girl as well, I will have her and the Elfaery tortured until their Crysterial Progression kills them then execute her precious Furyvire.'

The Jester feigned shock,

'How sinister of you!' laughed the Jester, 'To do such a thing to a woman, shame on you!'

'She and what is inside her are a great threat to my claim to the Darkaenian Supremacy,' said Xeropheers, 'They need to be disposed of.'

'Good luck!' singsong the Jester as he laughed maniacally and disappeared behind the throne which Xeropheers claimed as his own.

Raevyria, Denavayda and Demethari, still bound and chained to each other, were escorted off *The Poisoned Duchess* by a dozen Darkaenian Soldiers and taken to the great hall where the Senate of Lord Corruptors and the new Supreme Corruptor were gathered.

'What do you intend to do to us?' asked Demethari as he, Raevyria and Denavayda were forced onto their knees.

'You three are to be punished for the murder of Supreme Corruptor Mortipher and his Heir Prince Zelderaph,' announced one of the Lord Corruptors.

'It's just as the Jester said,' mused Demethari,

'SILENCE!' commanded Xeropheers. The great hall fell silent. 'My father was tricked and killed by these filthy Crysteors--'

'I'm not a Crysteor, Furyvires can't be Crysteors,' interrupted Denavayda. Raevyria and Demethari looked at him incredulously, which Denavayda quickly noticed, 'What? It's true,'

'I said silence! Impudent fools.' said Xeropheers impatiently as he rose from his throne and approached Raevyria, Demethari and Denavayda, 'You will pay for murdering Mortipher and Zelderaph,' The Lord Corruptors exchanged uneasy looks at one another, 'For your crimes against the Darkaenian Supremacy I hereby sentence the three of you to public torture and execution.' Raevyria, Demethari and Denavayda looked exasperated,

'You can't be serious,' said Denavayda,

'You're an evil piece of work, aren't you?' said Demethari angrily,

'Xeropheers please don't do this,' said Raevyria desperately, 'You don't have to--' but before Raevyria could finish Xeropheers punched her to the ground,

'Shut up, stupid girl,' hissed Xeropheers, 'The three of you will be taken to the dungeons for interrogation before facing your fate in the Horrordrome. Take them away.' At Xeropheers' command the Darkaenian Soldiers pulled Raevyria, Denavayda and Demethari up onto their feet and began to drag them towards the doors of the great hall.

'This is not good,' said Demethari worriedly, 'Our situation is more dire than I thought.' Dire? Although her head was throbbing from Xeropheers' punch, that word, dire, it made Raevyria remember what Dreameus and Nighthier had said to her.

'*If you are ever in a dire situation and need any help, just hold that flower, call our names and we'll come and help you, but we can only do this once, okay?*'

'*One flower, one chance. Don't waste it.*'

As the Darkaenian Soldiers were dragging Raevyria, Demethari and Denavayda towards the doors of the great hall, Raevyria used her Onceway to destroy the chains that bound her, Denavayda and Demethari together and raised her flower up in the air,

'NIGHTHIER! DREAMEUS!' shouted Raevyria as her voice reverberated throughout the great hall. A few awkward moments of awkward silence passed as Xeropheers, the Senate of Lord Corruptors, the Darkaenian Soldiers, Denavayda and Demethari looked at Raevyria bewildered. Nothing happened.

'What are you doing, Raevyria?' asked Demethari curiously,

'Raevyria, are you alright?' Denavayda asked concerned.

'Did you really expect something to happen!?' laughed Xeropheers, 'You stupid, stupid girl.' Xeropheers then unsheathed his handheld crossbow and fired an arrow at Raevyria's head. The arrow pierced Raevyria's forehead, and the impact of the shot made her fall backwards. Denavayda caught Raevyria and knelt to the ground with her in his arms. He pulled the arrow out of Raevyria's forehead and gently tried to shake her awake.

'Raevyria, wake up,' said Denavayda softly as he stroked her face, 'Come on wake up,' but Raevyria did not respond. Denavayda glared at Xeropheers while the new Supreme Corruptor laughed and chuckled to himself,

'Finish them, FINISH THEM!' commanded Xeropheers. At the Supreme Corruptor'ss command, the Darkaenian Soldiers unsheathed their own handheld crossbows and began to fire at Denvayda, Raevyria and Demethari.

'NO!' shouted Denavayda as he used his majestic wings to create an impenetrable shield around himself and the unconscious Raevyria. The arrows bounced off Denavayda's wings as if they were nothing. Demethari, wandless, used his Onceway to create a protective barrier around himself and the arrows disappeared into nothingness upon impact. Xeropheers and the Lord Corruptors began to summon ethereal streams of Sinscourge from their bodies and projected them at Demethari, Denavayda and Raevyria. Demethari began to defend himself, Denavayda and Raevyria from the streams of Sinscourge but he quickly weakened as his Crysterial Progression consumed the rest of his body. Demethari fell to the ground, panting and wheezing in pain. He could barely contain the protective barrier around himself.

Inside the protective dome created by his wings, Denavayda stroked Raevyria's cheek, held her close and looked at the Look-At-Me-Not that lay withered in her hand. To Denavayda's surprise, the flower disappeared into dust and two wisps of Onceway emerged from Raevyria's body.

Xeropheers once again ordered the Darkaenian Soldiers and the Senate of Lord Corruptors to finish them off. The Darkaenian Soldiers unsheathed their swords and began to charge at Demethari, Denavayda and Raevyria while the Lord Corruptors conjured their darkness and shot streams of Sinscourge at the trio. The Darkaenian Soldiers and the Sinscourge were within inches of reaching Raevyria, Denavayda and Demethari when Nighthier and Dreameus appeared from the wisps of Onceway and engaged the forces that opposed them.

Chapter Ten

A Miracle and a Monster

With his war scythe that he conjured from within himself, Nighthier charged towards the Darkaenian Soldiers and smoothly took them out with his Onceway, impressive athleticism and swordsmanship skills, while Dreameus, with his own war scythe, effortlessly used his Onceway to destroy the currents of ethereal Sinscourge that threatened Raevyria, Denavayda and Demethari.

The Supreme Corruptor was shocked at what he was witnessing; these two teenage boys that had, quite literally, appeared out of nowhere, facilely took down the Darkaenian Soldiers and the combined power of the Senate of Lord Corruptors and himself.

'You!' raged Xeropheers as he unsheathed his longsword and marched towards Nighthier, who had just finished dispatching the last of the Darkaenian soldiers. Wordlessly, Nighthier approached Xeropheers and, with a swift motion of his war scythe, he sliced the new Supreme Corruptor across the face, blinding him in his left eye, and kicked him to the ground as Xeropheers began to profusely bleed black ooze from his face, screaming. As Nighthier was dealing with Xeropheers, Dreameus handled the Senate of Lord Corruptors by encasing them inside golden iridescent crystal they could neither see nor break out of.

While Nighthier and Dreameus were fighting their battles with Xeropheers and the Senate of Lord Corruptors respectively, Raevyria regained consciousness and asked what was going on. To answer her question, Denavayda tucked his wings away and allowed Raevyria to watch the fights. She was both shocked and in awe by what Nighthier and Dreameus were capable of. Raevyria watched in amazement as the two boys fought against the soldiers and the Lord Corruptor's Sinscourge and was taken aback by their unusual Onceway; Nighthier's Onceway appeared to be tainted by pearlescent darkness while Dreameus' power illuminated a golden iridescent light. She was also happy that they were true to their word and that they came to help her when called.

After dealing with the Supreme Corruptor and the Senate of Lord Corruptors, Nighthier and Dreameus approached Raevyria, Denavayda and Demethari.

'Everyone alright?' asked Dreameus concerned as he bent down in front of Raevyria and examined the crystal scar on her forehead, 'Crysterial Progression…a blessing and a curse, am I right?'

'Nighthier, Dreameus, thank you for coming,' said Raevyria gratefully,

'It's not over yet,' said Nighthier coldly, 'No doubt this place is crawling with Darkaenian Soldiers,'

'Don't worry,' said Dreameus reassuringly as he saw the concerned look on Raevyria's face, 'As long as the five of us stick together, I'm sure we'll be fine.' Raevyria, Denavayda and Demethari looked at each other surprised, that was exactly what Jester had said to them the last time he saw them. Dreameus turned to Demethari and examined his Crysterial Progression. Dreameus took the elderly Elfaery's hands into his own and closed his eyes. After a few moments, the crystal on Demethari's face began to regress and his hands returned to normal. Demethari looked at his hands and felt his crystal-free face for the first time in a very long time. Raevyria gasped in shock at what Dreameus had done, even Denavayda looked impressed. 'I haven't cured it,' said Dreameus quickly, 'I've just given you a bit more time, if anyone deserves a second chance it's you Demethari.'

'Thank you,' said Demethari gratefully as tears welled up in his eyes, 'Thank you so much, who are you both?'

'This is Dreameus,' said Raevyria as she stroked Dreameus' cheek, 'And this is Nighthier.' Raevyria smiled as she held out a hand to Nighthier. Unlike Dreameus, who accepted the gesture, Nighthier refused to take Raevyria's hand.

'If you are feeling rested, we should go,' said Nighthier coldly as Dreameus helped Raevyria to her feet.

'What about him?' asked Dreameus curiously as he gestured to Xeropheers, who was still screaming and writhing in pain.

'We could finish him off here, or leave him in his suffering,' said Nighthier casually, 'What do you think?' Nighthier looked at Raevyria. Raevyria thought long and hard about it, even though she really wanted Xeropheers dead for taking Zelderaph away from her the thought of him suffering made her feel better.

'Leave him in his suffering,' said Raevyria coldly, 'He is not worth killing.'

'…If you say so,' said Nighthier grumpily, disappointed Raevyria had spared Xeropheers' life.

'Oh, by the way, I think you guys might need these,' said Dreameus as he snapped his fingers and conjured Denavayda's swords Tongue and Tooth, as well as Raevyria's and Demethari's wands.

'Does that not hurt you? Using the Onceway wandless?' asked Raevyria concerned,

'No, not really,' said Dreameus thoughtfully,

'You must be very powerful,' said Demethari in awe of Dreameus,

'I wouldn't say that exactly,' said Dreameus modestly, 'But mine and Nighthier's circumstances are kind of unique,'

'What do you mean?' asked Raevyria. Both Nighthier and Dreameus gazed at Raevyria.

'Isn't it obvious yet?' asked Nighthier bewildered. Raevyria looked baffled, 'Never mind, I guess you'll find out sooner or later.'

At that moment, Darkaenian Soldiers flooded the great hall and surrounded Raevyria, Denavayda, Demethari, Nighthier and Dreameus, wielding ebony broadswords.

'Dream? Are you ready?' whispered Nighthier to his brother,

'I'm ready whenever you are, Night,' Dreameus whispered back. Suddenly, the Darkaenian Soldiers began to charge at the five. With his nodachi sword in hand, Nighthier swung his blade and knocked several Darkaenian Soldiers backwards. He then summoned ethereal streams of black Onceway from his body, which he used to engulf many of the Darkaenian Soldiers and transformed them into monstrous Sinscourged covered in black crystal. With the Sinscourged under his control, Nighthier commanded them to kill, and they began to kill the Darkaenian Soldiers. Dreameus, with his golden Onceway, levitated many of the Darkaenian Soldiers into the air and forcefully crushed them with his powers. Denavayda used his pyromancy to incinerate the Darkaenian Soldiers and engaged in close combat with several of them, using a mixture of impressive swordsmanship and martial prowess. Raevyria and Demethari used their wands to destroy the Darkaenian Soldiers that surrounded them. Once the Darkaenian Soldiers were disposed of, Dreameus used his powers to destroy the Sinscourged Nighthier had created.

After dispatching the Darkaenian Soldiers, the five of them, led by Denavayda, made their way out of the great hall and, once they reached outside the Darkaenian Palace, they found themselves surrounded by the entire Darkaenian army of Soldiers and Sinscourged.

'This isn't good,' mused Demethari, 'We cannot defeat them all.'

'Well, we can give it a good go,' said Denavayda coolly and he tightened his grip on Tongue and Tooth.

'No, Demethari's right,' said Raevyria, 'We can't handle all of these things.'

'It's a shame we don't have any train tickets,' mused Nighthier, '*The Locomystic* would be very covenient right now,'

'I think we're going to have to retreat,' said Dreameus as he cast a barrier around the group, 'To Sacregard!' Dreameus shouted and, in a flash of light, the five found themselves in the Courtyard of the Crystaverse in Sacregard.

'Remarkable,' gasped Demethari, fascinated by Nighthier and sDreameus' power,

'Thank you Nighthier, Dreameus,' said Raevyria gratefully, 'You both really saved our lives.'

'Glad we could help,' smiled Dreameus,

'Yeah, it was no problem,' said Nighthier. At that moment, both Nighthier and Dreameus began to slowly fade away.

'What's happening?' asked Raevyria worriedly as she rushed to the boys and grabbed hold of Nighthier and Dreameus' hands.

'Our time has been spent,' said Dreameus,

'One flower, one chance, remember?' said Nighthier.

'Don't worry, you'll see us again,' said Dreameus reassuringly, 'However we won't remember anything.'

'Why won't you remember?' asked Raevyria sadly. Dreameus and Nighthier smiled weakly, and, with their free hands, they placed them on Raevyria's tummy.

'Because we've not been born yet,' said Nighthier and Dreameus together. A look of realization appeared on Raevyria's face as Demethari and Denavayda looked surprised,

'That's impossible!' gasped Demethari, 'No Crysteor has ever had children before!'

'Well, Zelderaph and Raevyria were able to do it,' said Nighthier,

'You two are-? Am I-?' stuttered Raevyria, who was beyond flabbergasted. Raevyria's eyes began to well up with tears as she realized she was pregnant and in the presence of her future sons. Dreameus leaned toward Raevyria and gave her a warm embrace.

'See you in a few months, mother,' whispered Dreameus softly as Raevyria cried and reciprocated the embrace.

'See you later,' said Nighthier as he and Dreameus finally faded away.

Raevyria, Demethari and Denavayda were left all alone in the Courtyard when Raevyria placed her hands on her abdomen and began to cry tears of happiness,

'I can't believe it,' she gasped, 'How is this possible?'

'It's a miracle,' said Demethari, 'This has never happened before!' Just as Denavayda was about to say something, the ground beneath them began to shake violently. The Prime Crysteor, Auraedeus Auramaedes, emerged from the Crystaverse, weakened and bleeding profusely from his chest. Raevyria, Demethari and Denavayda rushed to the Prime Crysteor and caught him as he collapsed in their arms.

'Prime Crysteor, what happened?' asked Demethari worriedly. The Prime Crysteor panted as he pulled Demethari closer and whispered something in his ear before passing out and triggering his Crysterial Progression.

'What did he say?' asked Raevyria curiously. Without saying a word, Demethari rose to his feet and made his way to the Crystaverse, with Raevyria and Denavayda closely following behind him.

Raevyria and Denavayda followed Demethari to the Gate Chamber and saw the Masters of the Crystaverse subduing a large, ferocious monster in chains made of the Onceway from their wands. Raevyria instantly recognized the monster as it was the very creature, she had had nightmares about in the past.

'DEMETHARI! Help us!' called one of the Masters as he struggled to maintain his hold over the monster,

'But how? I thought the Gate of Neverearth was empty!' exclaimed Raevyria,

'I believe I have some explaining to do,' said Demethari, 'Do you remember three years ago when the Darkaenians were sighted and the Prime Crysteor summoned the Masters to the Gate Chamber? Well, we were anxious that the Darkaenians would penetrate the barrier and somehow find their way into the Crystaverse so the Prime Crysteor sealed the Beast of the Beyond within himself and kept it within him in case the Darkaenians found their way to the Gate Chamber, which is exactly what happened the other day when Mortipher corrupted me to show him the Gate Chamber. Once we had shown the Darkaenians the Gate was empty the Prime Crysteor was going to return the Beast of the Beyond to its prison, but it appears as though the Beast of the Beyond is putting up quite a fight after being extracted from the Prime Crysteor.'

'How reckless!' snapped Denavayda angrily, 'He could've killed everyone!'

'Now is not the time to discuss the actions of the Prime Crysteor!' said Demethari urgently, 'Raevyria, help me and the Masters in imprisoning the Beast once again!'

'You expect her to help in her condition!?' said Denavayda incredulously, 'No, she's not doing it she--' Before Denavayda could even finish his sentence Raevyria brushed past him and Demethari and contributed her efforts to imprison the Beast of the Beyond. With her wands, she created her own chains of Onceway and bound the Beast within them. Demethari immediately lent his power to the cause and aided his fellow Masters in returning the Beast of the Beyond to the Gate of Neverearth.

The Beast of the Beyond was putting up a fight and was not going to return to the Gate of Neverearth quietly. The Beast of the Beyond roared with anger as it spat large amounts of Sinscourge from its mouth and tried to hit the Masters with it, but the Beast failed to do so as each of the Masters, including Raevyria, were protected by defensive fire barriers created by Denavayda. After creating fire barriers for the Masters of the Crystaverse, Denavayda flew to the top of the Beast of the Beyond and hit it with large balls of fire from his fists, forcing the snapping monster downwards into the Gate of Neverearth. After a long and painful struggle, the Beast of the Beyond entered the schism of space and time that was Neverearth and the Gate began to slowly close behind it.

As the Gate was closing the Beast of the Beyond began to talk.

'**Accursed Crysteors**,' growled the Beast, '**This seal, this Gate, will not confine me forever. I will bring you such suffering you will beg for death. One day, the Destructor and the Maker will determine the fate of your precious Foreverearth and I shall rise again**.'

'Oh, do shut up,' said Demethari impatiently as the Gate closed and began to lock itself.

Demethari turned to Raevyria and smiled at her weakly.

'My dear girl,' said Demethari softly as he stroked his hand on Raevyria's cheek. 'I am so happy for you, and so proud of you…' Demethari smiled weakly but before he could say anything the sound of a single round of applause was heard in the Gate Chamber, following the sound Raevyria, Demethari and the Masters saw it was the Jester,

'Bravo Crysteors, bravo!' cheered the Jester, 'You subdued the Beast, AGAIN! A tiresome job this sealing business! So, who is going to maintain it this time?!'

'I think you know that Jester,' said Demethari sullenly. Raevyria looked at Demethari confused,

'Noble Demethari, brave Demethari, are you going to do it this time Demethari?' chuckled Jester as he cartwheeled to the old Elfaery's side.

'What do you mean?' asked Raevyria,

'It is my turn to strengthen the seal,' said Demethari. Raevyria shook her head,

'No, you can't,' said Raevyria as tears began to well up in her eyes, 'You'll die if you do.'

'I think that is the reason why Dreameus took most of my Crysterial Progression away,' said Demethari, 'I think he knew I wanted to be of help, so he took away my Crysterial Progression so I could be strong enough to sacrifice myself to the seal…'

'Please don't!' cried Raevyria, 'Please, I'm going to become a mother, you have to meet my children and-'

'I have already met them Raevyria,' said Demethari reassuringly, 'And they are fine young men. I am so happy for you and so proud of you, my dear Raevyria. Please remember everything I taught you, and always follow your heart. Promise me?'

'I promise,' Raevyria wept as the elderly Elfaery wrapped his arms around her and gave her a gentle kiss on the forehead.

'Goodbye, dear Raevyria,' said Demethari as a tear trickled down his face and he began to glow and disappear into dust. The dust settled down on the Gate of Neverearth until it was absorbed and the intermittent glowing of the Gate stopped.

Raevyria fell to her knees sobbing. Denavayda approached her, bent down beside her, and held her in a tight, warm embrace. The Jester began to mock Raevyria for crying and Denavayda scowled at him for it. The Masters surrounded Raevyria and Denavayda,

'Is it true? Are you really with child?' asked one of the Masters. Raevyria lookedup and nodded her head. The Masters began to chat amongst themselves, astonished.

'It appears the vultures wish to feed on your little miracles,' whispered Jester as he pressed his head against Raevyria's and looked warningly at the gossiping Masters, 'But they are not the only ones. Xeropheers will chase you and hunt you down for what is growing inside of you, he cannot be the true Supreme Corruptor until Zelderaph's last gifts are disposed of.'

'What should I do?' Raevyria whispered back, loud enough for both Jester and Denavayda to hear.

'We should leave,' whispered Denavayda, 'You and me, let's leave and not come back.'

'*We*?' asked Raevyria surprised, 'No Denavayda, I cannot put you in danger and-'

'Let the Furyvire do what he wants!' said Jester in sing-song as he jumped to his feet and spun on the spot, 'The adventures of Raevyria and Denavayda!

Sounds fun, go for it! Don't forget to send me a postcard!' The Jester laughed as he then disappeared into nothingness.

As the Masters were talking amongst themselves, Raevyria and Denavayda took each other's hands and slowly crept out of the Gate Chamber and made their way across the Courtyard and to the stables, where Scorch was waiting for them.

'Are you sure you want to do this?' asked Raevyria, 'Running from the Darkaenian Supremacy and the Crystaverse... this could be dangerous and-'

'I don't care,' said Denavayda softly as he stroked his hand across Raevyria's cheek and smiled, 'I'm coming with you; besides, someone needs to keep you and those kids out of trouble.' Raevyria laughed and gave Denavayda a kiss on the cheek,

'Thank you, Denavayda,' said Raevyria sweetly as she mounted Scorch, rode out of the stables and, with a mighty flap of Scorch's wings, the Starbird ascended into the air and towards the rising light of Sol'Astriel, with Denavayda flying closely behind.

Printed in Dunstable, United Kingdom

66324801R00085